Keeping My Prince Charming

J. S. Cooper

Thank you for reading Keeping My Prince Charming. Please join my mailing list
to receive updates on new books.

Keeping My Prince Charming should be read after Finding My Prince Charming and Taming My Prince Charming.
It is the final book in the Prince Charming series.

TABLE OF CONTENTS

PROLOGUE

Sex. Love. Lies. Secrets. Money. That's my world now. That's the world I've found myself in. I feel a bit like Alice in Wonderland, spinning around and discombobulated. Up is down and down is up. Nothing makes sense and yet it all makes absolute sense. I never would have believed that I, Lola Franklin, would have found myself in a world of fairytales. Maybe that's because I didn't believe they existed. And I wasn't wrong. At least, not the fairytales that Disney spins us. They don't exist completely. However, one thing is true: I did meet my Prince Charming. My very own imperfect Prince Charming.

Every woman wants to meet her Prince Charming. She wants a man who will sweep her off of her feet. She wants a man who will love her above everyone else. She wants a man who will love her as if he couldn't live without her. She wants a man who can think of no one but her. Yes, every woman wants a Prince Charming. The real question is: how do you find, tame and keep him? That is the question that we all want answered. Finding a great guy is only part of the battle. It's the taming and the keeping of the guy that're the real challenge. And it's an even bigger challenge if that man is Xavier Van Romerius.

CHAPTER ONE
LOLA

"Let me touch you. Let me stir the passions in your soul until they became a storm of desire. I want your waves to crash down all over me. I want your rain to pour in my mouth. I want to feel your body move to the earthquake inside. I want to make your volcano erupt on top of me so that I don't even remember where I end and you begin." Casper stepped toward me with a threatening smile, his hands outstretched, and I blanched at his gaze. What was I doing here, in this room, with this man— this man whose words made a mockery of the beauty of lovemaking?

There was a stirring in my stomach as I stood in the cold, poorly lit room. I could hear the sounds of music playing in other parts of the palace. There were bursts of laughter, and all I could wonder was if they were laughing at me. Lola Franklin, the American slut fiancée of Prince Xavier of Romerius. My cheeks burned in shame as I stared at Casper, his handsome face gazing at me as if I were his Sunday dinner and he was very, very hungry.

There's always a moment in life that makes you question your sanity. Sometimes it lasts longer than others. Sometimes it's gone in a blip of time. Often, that moment seems to stop time. Like now. I felt like time had stopped as I stood there with Casper and the traitor.

"So, what do you say?" Casper looked at me with dark eyes full of desire. "I promise we can give you more pleasure than you've ever experienced." His voice was melodic and sensual, as if trying to seduce me with its sound alone. The sound was calming to my body and I felt a tingling between my legs as I stared at his virile body, so obviously wanting me. His arms were strong and muscular and, for a brief second, I imagined him on top of me, pinning my arms back as he took me roughly. Casper was a man who would dominate me and take what he wanted with precision. "Are you thinking of how much pleasure I can give you, Lola?" He stepped forward again, his fingers lightly brushing my hair off of my shoulder as he bent down and kissed the skin next to my collarbone softly. His lips were warm and firm, and I froze. Everything about this moment was so wrong, but my body was expectant, waiting, and defiant. My body wanted to let him take me so I could get back at Xavier. I felt like this was my chance to make him hurt as he had hurt me.

"*We* can make this the best night of your life." Casper gazed into my eyes expectantly and then leaned toward my ear and blew gently. His breath tickled my ear and I felt a thrill of excitement run through my body unexpectedly. My body was reacting to him, even though my brain wanted nothing to do with him. Then I felt the tip of his tongue running down my neck. He licked back up and I felt his tongue on my lips. I gasped as he smirked at me, his eyes sparkling into mine as he dared me to let him continue. "I can give you more pleasure than you believed possible. Let me take you on a journey. Let *us* take you on a journey," he said huskily and I jumped back suddenly.

His words broke me out of my reverie and I looked past him to the figure by the door.

"No, no, and no." My voice was loud as I answered his questions, but faced right. "And you, Tarquin, how could you?" My voice caught as I stared at Xavier's cousin. "I thought we were friends?"

"We are friends. I want to be more than friends, though." He licked his lips and I shivered as he stepped toward me with a glint in his eyes. "Don't you think I'm handsome?"

"Tarquin!" I chastised him. "Where is this coming from? You know I'm engaged to Xavier."

"Yeah, right." He laughed and then looked at Casper uncertainly. I looked at Casper, whose face had changed to a grimace and I knew he was responsible for Tarquin's entrance into the room.

"What game are you playing?" My voice was tight as I stared at him. "Why are you here, Tarquin?"

"My brother asked me to—"

"Your brother?" My jaw dropped. "Casper is your brother?"

"Yes." He nodded, looking more and more unsure of himself.

"So Casper is Xavier's cousin as well?"

"You're smarter than you look." Casper gazed at me with a sneer.

"Excuse me?" I frowned at his tone.

"Casper." Tarquin spoke up. "That was rude. Lola doesn't deserve to be talked to like that."

"Tarquin," Casper said, turning to him, "you're lucky that you're even here. You know, technically, it's against the rules for you to be here."

"You're the one that told me to come." Tarquin looked annoyed but unsure of himself.

"Didn't you tell me that you liked her?" Casper looked me up and down. "Didn't you tell me you wished that you had a chance with her?"

"Casper." Tarquin blushed. "Why are you saying all of this?"

"Isn't it true? Isn't this what you wanted?" Casper's lip curled. "Isn't this the girl?"

"Casper." Tarquin's eyes flashed at his brother murderously and I wondered what Casper was talking about. Had Tarquin talked about me to his brother? What had he said? I hadn't gotten any vibes from Tarquin that he'd been interested in me. He couldn't possibly be interested in me, could he?

"So what're you going to do, Lola?" Casper turned toward me. "Stick with the prince you know wants you? Or wait around for Xavier? Xavier, the man that's probably fucking Violeta as we speak."

"You're disgusting." I shook my head, finally coming out of my shock and haze. "How could you do this to me?" I turned to Tarquin. "After everything...I thought we were friends." I looked into his eyes and let him see my unveiled hurt and pain. He deserved to see how much he'd hurt me.

"Lola." Xavier's voice was loud as he shouted down the corridor. "Lola, where are you?"

"I'm in here, Xavier," I cried out and ran to the door. "I'm in here." I opened the door and Xavier stood there in front of me, his eyes distraught as he looked me over.

"What's going on in here?" He looked behind me at Casper and Tarquin and then at my ashen face. "Are you okay, Lola?"

"I'd like to go home, please," I whispered, my voice shaking. I didn't want him to ask me what had happened or what was going to happen. I didn't want him to know that for one split second, I had been considering going along with Casper. Not because I liked Casper or wanted him, but because I was hurt and confused and jealous. I closed my eyes for a second, wishing that I was back home in Florida. All of a sudden, my mundane life didn't seem so trite and boring. I'd give anything for boring right now. I'd give anything to be away from here and these men. All of whom were looking at me with a mixture of lust, distaste, worry, concern and anger. This wasn't what my experience in Europe was meant to be like.

This wasn't meant to be my love story: stripping in front of a group of men, swinging my hips, touching my breasts. My face reddened at the memories. I just wanted to die. Or be magically swept away from this place.

"Let's go." Xavier grabbed my arm, his eyes bleak as he turned towards Casper. "I expected better from you."

"Better from me?" Casper laughed, his voice unashamed and arrogant. "Who do you think you are? Prince Charming come to rescue his Cinderella or Sleeping Beauty?"

"I don't think Sleeping Beauty here gets much sleep," Tarquin joked, and Xavier turned toward him.

"You were like a brother to me, Tarquin. I'm so disappointed in you." Xavier's voice dropped to a low murmur, and Tarquin's face twisted in confusion and pain.

"I wasn't doing anything to hurt you," he whispered, unsure of himself now. He looked towards his brother for backup, but all Casper could do was stand there and smirk.

"Stop being all high and mighty, Xavier." Violeta suddenly appeared at the door and her face looked hurt. "Why don't you tell Lola who you really are?"

"Who I really am?"

"Why don't you tell her about us?"

"She knows that we dated and that you mean nothing to me."

"Does she know about the baby you made me give up? Does she know why you went to London?"

"Baby?" I gasped, all color fleeing my face as I took in her words and looked at Xavier's darkening expression.

"She's lying," Xavier said, his voice tight.

"Does this look like I'm lying?" Violeta walked over to me and I watched as she flipped through her phone and showed me a photo of her in what appeared to be a hospital bed with a baby. A newborn baby. Violeta's face looked stressed and loving as she gazed at the baby. It was evident from her expression in the photo that she'd loved the baby.

"Xavier?" I looked at him with wide eyes.

"Lola." He blinked at me, his face looking angry.

"Is that your son?"

"It's his." Violeta grabbed my arm. "Do you really want to be with a man that would so callously leave the mother of his child? He made me give my son away. That is why I'm bitter. That is why I want to take him down. That is why I want to expose him for who he is. He's not a prince of the people.

He's a prince that …" Violeta's voice trailed off at Xavier's expression.

"Do you really want to play this game?" Xavier looked at Violeta. "Do you want to go down this road, with me?"

"Don't threaten Violeta." Casper stepped forward. "We will expose you, Xavier."

"I wouldn't throw stones, Casper." Xavier's voice was soft. "You know what they say about people who live in glass houses. I wouldn't want everything to come crashing down on top of you."

"Who do you think you are?" Casper's face contorted as he stared at Xavier, and all of his charm and good looks disappeared in an instant.

"Let's go, Lola." Xavier sighed deeply and we exited the room in silence. He stopped briefly in the corridor, pulled his jacket off and handed it to me. "Wear this," he said stiffly, and he watched as I pulled it on and buttoned it up quickly. We continued walking in silence until we made our way outside and a valet pulled up to the front with a car. "Get in," he said, his tone still low and his eyes dark. I knew that he was upset with me, and was probably questioning what I'd been doing in the room. I felt like it was a double standard. Why was he allowed to be mad at me when he had been with Violeta? Why was he the one who was acting like he was wronged when Violeta had just dropped a bomb on me?

The car pulled away and I sat back, shivering in the seat, feeling more alone than I'd ever felt in my life. And then something snapped in me. This wasn't my fault. I wasn't the bad person here.

"So you're just going to ignore me?" I turned towards Xavier, fuming in my anger. "Don't you think you owe me an explanation?"

"I don't think I'm ignoring you." His lips curled up as he stared at me. "I'm taking you home, aren't I?"

"In silence," I huffed. "And when you do talk to me it's with an attitude."

"Att-i-tude?" he said slowly and deliberately. "I have an attitude?"

"Yes, you do. Stop acting like I'm some whore or plaything." I turned away from him. "I didn't ask for this."

"What do you want from me, Lola?" He asked so softly that I barely heard him.

"I want you to be a prince." I shrugged, suddenly embarrassed to tell him everything I was thinking. I wanted him to tell me that he was sorry for this whole mess and that he wanted to start again. I wanted him to tell me that this was all a dream or some weird test or anything other than what it was.

"I am a prince," he said simply. He gazed at me then, his eyes traveling down my body, noticing my uncomfortable slouch and tense shoulders. "I'm not a Prince Charming, though, Lola. They don't exist. At least I don't know any princes that would fit into fairytales." His fingers caressed the top of my head. "Real life isn't a Disney cartoon."

"I never said it was." I bit my lower lip to stop it from trembling.

"I'm not going to ride up on my white horse and whisk you away to a castle." He rolled his eyes. "This isn't some magical ride, and the world of royalty isn't something to be envied and fantasized about. I mean, there is a ride I can take you on, but it will be very bumpy, if you know what I mean." He paused and licked his lips as he stared at me. "Though, I've heard bumpy rides are the most enjoyable."

"I never fantasized about being royalty." I moved away from him, annoyed at his assumption. It was true that I'd never been someone that had any aspirations to become a part of the aristocracy, but I'd be lying if I didn't admit that a small part of me had dreamed of being swept away and wooed by a prince. Who didn't want a man to love and cherish them? Who didn't want to be taken on a magical ride of love?

"This world—my world—is dark and deep and sinister. There are no happy endings. No fairytales. No knights in shining armor. There are just men that have titles and men that have money. And there are some men, like me, that have both, money and titles. We're all just human. We're not gods. We're just like regular people, but we play more dangerous games. I am not the father of Violeta's baby. This is part of her game to intimidate you to leave me. This is just the start of the games that we will find ourselves in."

"What games?"

"You really want to know, Lola? You really want to be exposed to that darkness?"

"You've already exposed me to it," I said softly, hugging his jacket around me tighter. "You already exposed me to Casper and I can't imagine it gets much darker than him."

"Then you can't imagine much." His eyes searched mine, and for a few seconds we just stared at each other in the darkness. "How do you think most of the royal families got into power, Lola? Do you think

God came down and said, 'I think you and you and you should rule the others'?"

"No."

"Have you seen *Game of Thrones?*"

"A few episodes." I nodded.

"That show is like my real life, Lola. Families fight and lie and backstab to get into power. That is how all the royal families in the world have gotten into power. Our history is deep and dark." He sat back. "And that is why I love art. I need color in my life. I need life. I need beauty. I need something that hasn't been spoiled by greed."

"That's why you love art so much?"

"Yes, that's why I love art. And that's why I'm an art professor." He sighed. "I want to know that, for at least part of my life, I lived for me."

"And the rest of your life...?" My voice trailed off as I stared at him, my brain ticking a hundred miles a minute. "The rest of your life you become a part of the darkness?"

"This is who I am, Lola." He turned to me and grabbed my hand. "I was so worried when I walked into that room. So worried that something had happened to you. I made a mistake by bringing you here. It was unfair to subject you to this life."

"What are you saying?" I frowned at the look in his eyes.

"I'm saying that I think you should go home."

"But what about the engagement?"

"It was fake. We both know that. It was a stupid idea. I shouldn't have taken advantage of your good nature. I just wanted to be with you. I wanted to see what we..." His voice trailed off and he looked away. "It's not important now."

"So that's it, then? After everything, that's it?"

"What do you want me to say?" He grabbed my hand. "You don't belong in this world."

"Because I'm a poor American?"

"No." His fingers gripped my hand tighter. "That has nothing to do with it."

"Then why?"

"Why do you even want to stay, after what just happened?"

"Because I like you," I said softly. What was so hard for him to understand? Didn't he get that I had come with him because I thought he was cute? That everything had been exciting for me because I liked him? I'd been attracted to him the first time I saw him in the museum. He'd been my sex god, and the fact that he had been attracted to me as well had ignited a feeling inside of me that I hadn't been able to quell.

"I'm not a good guy to like." He frowned.

"You could become a good guy to like."

"You think it's that easy?" He cocked his head and surveyed my face, then smirked. "You're so young and naive, Lola. I will never become a good guy."

"Maybe I don't want a good guy." I shrugged, my eyes never leaving his. "Maybe I want a guy that can take me on an adventure and never let me go."

"Do you really think you can handle that, Lola?" His green eyes looked at me skeptically. "Do you really think you're prepared for an adventure that has no guarantee of a happy ending?"

"When does anything have a guarantee of a happy ending?" I answered him honestly as I thought back to my past relationships and heartbreaks. I liked Xavier, and even though I didn't know what game he was playing, I still wanted to get to know him better. He intrigued me and infuriated me, but I couldn't walk away from him. Not now and not yet. Not after everything we'd been through.

"Very true." He gazed at me and then turned away. "We can talk again tomorrow. Tonight has been too much drama. You're overwhelmed and don't know what you're saying. Tomorrow we can decide where we want to go from here."

"Okay," I whispered, feeling worried. His words sounded ominous, and I was scared that he was going to tell me that I was going to have to leave. But that wasn't what scared me the most. What scared me was that as much as I didn't want to leave, another part of me really wanted to go. I wanted to leave and go back to London and pretend that I'd never met Xavier Van Romerius before in my life. And that was something that saddened me more than anything.

CHAPTER TWO
XAVIER

I didn't realize how easy it was to be a murderer. I didn't know how easy it was to have murderous thoughts. That was until tonight. Tonight I knew how easy it could be to kill someone. I knew that because I'd wanted to kill Casper and Tarquin when I'd seen them in the room with Lola. My gentle, sweet, unassuming Lola. She'd so nearly been taken advantage of by my two cousins, and I would have done anything to make them pay for what they'd done. I was so angry with them and with myself. I wondered what I'd been thinking to expose her to this world of depravity and sin. She was too young, too inexperienced, too naive and willing. I'd made a mistake in bringing her to Romerius. I'd made a mistake trying to have her be a part of my world. It was too dark, too sinister, too full of debauchery for her. She wasn't ready for the life that I lived. And I knew that I couldn't allow her to become even more entrenched in the games that we played.

Casper and Tarquin had known exactly what they were doing. I felt sorry for Tarquin. He was too young, and too easily influenced by his brother. He was a boy, trying to be a man, and he'd gotten caught up. It wasn't his fault, though I didn't consider that to be an excuse. I wouldn't be able to forgive him. And I'd have to speak to Sebastian about Tarquin's behavior. They'd have to cut ties. I was not going to allow anyone in my immediate circle be influenced by Casper and Violeta. Not at all. Not when I had so much to lose. And I knew that I couldn't lose Lola. Not now. Not when everything inside of me was telling me that she was the one. The only problem was that I didn't know if I wanted to have a 'one'. What did that mean for my life? What did that mean for my plans? What good could I bring to Lola's life? Maybe I'd brought enough trouble as it was. Maybe the best thing I could do would be to let her go. But everything in me rebelled at that thought. I unclenched my fists as I walked into my study, locked the door shut, and walked over to my desk. I stared at the invitation sitting on my planner and sat down in my leather chair. I picked it up and closed my eyes. I had a decision to make and I had no idea what to do. I opened my eyes and stared at the words, printed in black on the ivory linen paper. There was a gold line around the edge of the paper that I knew to be real gold. I had two days to make a decision. Two days that would change my life forever. Two days that would not only decide my fate, but Lola's as well.

Chapter Three
Lola

My heart felt heavy as I sat in the bathtub full of salts and oils. I played with the bubbles and watched as my fingers swished the water back and forth. The movement was slightly comforting and it helped me to forget the situation I found myself in. Xavier was right, he was not the Prince Charming I had always dreamed of. He was not a man who could take me away from my mundane world and make everything in my life perfect. If anything, he needed someone to take him away from his world. It was so dark and unbelievable, so coarse and uncaring. And most of all, it was lonely. I always thought that rich people and royalty had to be worried about gold diggers and people using them for their money. I always thought that their biggest worries came from not knowing who they could trust among their poorer and non-noble friends. Now I knew differently. Now I knew that their other rich friends were even worse. The games they played with each other and others were almost inhumane. I thought back to Casper and Tarquin and their proposition for a threesome. How could they have done that, knowing or at least thinking I was engaged to their cousin? Didn't they have any shame? I could still see the desire in Casper's eyes and the challenge. He hadn't been embarrassed at all. He had no hesitation, either. If he could have taken me to his bed and had his way with me, he would have. He wouldn't have cared. I would have been his conquest and he wouldn't have cared if he'd hurt his cousin. Tarquin, I knew, had more hesitation. He'd looked unsure and also slightly guilty, but that was probably because he was younger.

"You swimming in there?" Xavier opened the door and peeked into the bathroom.

"Obviously not," I said haughtily as I looked up at him from the tub, trying not to devour his face as I gazed at him.

"You're taking a long time," he said, walking into the bathroom completely.

"Is that a problem?" I slid down in the bath as he attempted to look at my breasts.

"No," he said simply with a wry smile as he sat on the toilet seat and gazed at me. "I was just making sure you hadn't fallen asleep."

"I'm not asleep." I smiled at him sweetly, my heart racing fast as he continued to stare at me. He was unnerving me with the warm look of concern on his face. He was no longer the angry and stone-faced Xavier of earlier.

"Good." He winked at me. "That would have made it awkward."

"Made what awkward?" I asked, confused.

"My making love to you."

"Oh." My face reddened.

"I do like waking my women up with sex, but only once I know they enjoy that." He grinned. "And I prefer it to be in the bed," he continued with a smirk as he licked his lips deliberately.

"I see." I blushed at his words. I kind of liked the idea of waking up with Xavier making love to me, but there was no way in hell I was going to tell him that.

"It's best if we're both alert." He grinned, stood up, and walked over to the bathtub and sat at the edge. He reached his fingers into the tub and splashed the water around slightly.

"What are you doing?" I asked him, my voice stammering as I watched him unbutton his shirt. His chest was playing peekaboo and I couldn't stop myself from staring at the expanse of skin on show, so tan and muscular. Xavier truly was a sex god. I just had to hand it to him. No matter what he was wearing, or where we were, he always had the ability to turn me on.

"I need to get clean as well." He licked his lips and threw his shirt onto the ground.

"There's not enough room in the tub for both of us." I gulped.

"There's always enough room for the two of us, Lola." He grinned and stood up, pulling his belt out of his pants and throwing it to the ground next to his shirt.

Then he stretched his arms up and I watched the rippling of his abs as I sat there. My fingers moved up to touch his stomach, but I stopped myself right at the last moment.

Xavier grinned down at me and started to unzip his pants. I moaned slightly as he pulled his pants down and I stared at his manhood, stiff and hard, and pointing directly toward me from his tight white briefs. I looked away so that I wasn't staring directly at his cock, and splashed myself with some water to cool off. Xavier was making this very difficult for me. Very, very difficult. How could I extricate myself from this situation when I still wanted to be with him so badly?

"What are you doing?" I gasped as he grabbed my hand and placed it on his manhood. His fingers squeezed mine as he stood there grinning down at me, our hands moving up and down his length.

"Getting ready for my bath."

"Get ready by yourself, please." I tried to move my hand away, but his grip tightened. "What are you doing?" I said again as I glared up at him.

"Letting you feel how hard you make me." He let go of my hand abruptly. "I want you to remember what you do to me, every single time you think of me."

"Ooh, wow, I'm so flattered," I said sarcastically. "What an honor it is to get you hard."

"Is that all you think this is?" His voice dropped as he stepped into the bathtub.

"Do I think my holding your cock is about making you horny and hard?" I asked and rolled my eyes. "What else should I think it's about? The cure to cancer?"

"Do you think it is so easy to make me hard?" His voice was a whisper as he reached down and pulled me up.

"What are you doing?" I gasped as his fingers slid down my arms to my hands as he lifted me. "Xavier," I protested as he pulled me towards him, my breasts rubbing bubbles all over his chest.

"Lola," he mocked me as his voice dropped to a sultry whisper and his hand rubbed bubbles down my back and to my ass.

"I didn't invite you to take a bath with me."

"And I don't need your invitation."

"You're such a pig."

"I know, I know. You've told me that about a million times." He squeezed my butt cheeks and pulled me against him harder.

"And I haven't forgotten any of the other times you said it, either."

"Then why do you keep acting so insufferable?"

"You think I'm insufferable?" He frowned. "Or are you just saying that?"

"Why would I just say that?" I rolled my eyes. "I don't say things I don't mean."

"So you mean to tell me that I'm insufferable?"

"Yeah."

"You know who I am?"

"Yeah."

"I should spank you for being impertinent."

"You think I'd let you get away with that?" I breathed out as I felt his hardness against my stomach.

"No." He smiled slyly. "And that's why it will be so good."

"Huh?" I said, confused. "Why will what be so good?"

"*It* will be fantastic." He breathed heavily. "Because you will try and slide away from me." His fingers gripped into the small of my back at the sides of my waist. "And when you slide away from me, you'll be squirming and wriggling like you are now." He bent down and whispered into my ear. "And that wiggling back and forth is very much turning me on." I paused as I realized my breasts were rubbing back and forth on his chest in an attempt to back away from him. And all that was succeeding in doing was making my nipples hard.

"I'm still mad at you." I glared at him. "What happened tonight, it's not okay. I don't know what sort of sick world you're a part of, but I don't appreciate being brought into it. I don't want to be part of some sick game you're playing with Violeta."

"Forget Violeta." His eyes narrowed and his face was full of distaste. "She means nothing to me. She is nothing. Casper and Tarquin will be dealt with as well."

"What are you going to do?" I asked softly, my heart thudding as I stared into his eyes. My body shivered slightly from being naked in the cool air above him, and he pulled me closer to him.

"Don't you worry your sweet head about it." His voice was dark. "I will take care of it."

"Are you still mad at me?" I asked, annoyed at myself for caring what he thought about me. This wasn't my fault and I shouldn't need his reassurance.

"I couldn't be mad at you, Lola. Mad at myself, yes. You? Never." He kissed the top of my head. "You did nothing wrong. It was you that was wronged. And I will make sure that Casper and Tarquin pay for what they did, even if it costs me everything."

"What are you talking about, Xavier?" I breathed out, suddenly feeling scared. What was he talking about? What would it cost him?

"Nothing right now." He lifted me out of the tub. "I'm done with talking. Right now all I want to be doing is making you scream."

"What are you doing?" I gasped as he bent me forward over the tub.

"What I wanted to do as soon as I walked into the bathroom." He grunted as he slipped some fingers in between my legs. "Taking what is mine."

"I'm not yours." I groaned as he rubbed my clit roughly.

"You will always be mine, Lola Franklin. You were mine from the first day that I saw you."

"The first day you saw me?" I moaned, and my body shuddered as I felt his cock entering me swiftly. "Xavier!" I screamed out his name as he grabbed me around my waist and shifted my butt back into him as he slammed into me. I felt his cock deep inside of me and I felt my body quaking as he filled me up so that I could feel every inch of him while he slid in and out of me. His fingers reached up and pinched my nipples and I writhed back against him, unable to stop myself from moving my body in rhythm with his. And then his right hand reached down and rubbed my clit gently as he fucked me. I closed my eyes and concentrated on the pleasure invading my body. I heard myself crying out as I came hard and fast. Yet, Xavier didn't stop moving inside of me or rubbing my clit. Instead he continued and within thirty seconds, I felt another orgasm building up again. This time, his hardness moved in and out of me slowly. Until suddenly he grunted and grabbed my hips and moved back and forth quickly, until he stopped abruptly and I felt his body shaking against mine as he exploded inside of me. He pulled out and then turned me towards him and kissed me hard.

"I told you you're mine." He kissed me on the lips again as his eyes bore down into mine. "Never forget that, Lola."

CHAPTER FOUR
XAVIER

I watched as Lola slept, and I marveled at how easily I'd come to my decision. She loved me. I'd seen it in her eyes when I'd gone into the bathroom. She loved me and I loved her. She was mine and I was going to risk everything to get my revenge. I was going to risk my heart for power. I'd seen the love that she had for me in her eyes. I knew that she wanted me. I knew that she was intrigued by me. I'd known it from the first time I'd seen her in the gallery. This wasn't what I'd planned on happening when I'd gone to London, but it felt like poetic justice. The timing couldn't have been more perfect. I was going to accept the invitation to the grand ball. I was going to accept it, and I was going to enter the challenge. I was going to become the most powerful man in Europe. I just had to make sure that I didn't sacrifice Lola's heart, or my own, for my second chance at power.

CHAPTER FIVE
LOLA

I arose before the sun and quickly packed up my things. My heart felt heavy as I gazed at a still sleeping Xavier. I was going to leave. I knew that I wasn't right for his world. I couldn't keep playing these games with him. I didn't want to feel used and unappreciated. I didn't want to be the woman who started accepting unacceptable behavior because I was so consumed by the feelings that exploded in my heart every time he smiled at me or said my name. I was Lola Franklin, for heaven's sake. I was the girl who had vowed never to let a man change who I was or what I would accept in a relationship. I wanted it all, or nothing at all. I wanted to be loved like nobody had been loved before. I wanted Xavier's sun to rise and fall with my smile. I wanted to be his world. I wanted him to look at me and feel like he couldn't go on without me by his side. I wanted to be his everything. The yin to his yang. The light to his darkness. I wanted to be *the one*. My heart ached for the want that struggled to remain silent in my heart. I crept toward the door softly, my brain not thinking about how I would leave the palace. I just needed to leave this room first. My heart raced as I edged closer and closer to the door. My hand reached for the doorknob, and I was about to turn it when I felt a hand on my back.

"Arrgh!" I screamed and turned around, my heart racing. "What are you doing?" I asked him, annoyed that he'd crept up on me. "I didn't even hear you behind me."

"I guess I can be quiet as a mouse as well," he said in a low growl, his eyes narrowed as he stared at me.

"What does that mean?" I squeaked out, my head dropping down his body and staring at him in all his naked glory. I swallowed hard as I took in his tan muscles and manhood. How glorious and perfect his body was. It wasn't fair. Not only was he handsome and sexy, but he also knew how to use every inch of what he had to make me feel like I was the only woman in the world when he made love to me. "Am I the Tom to your Jerry, or are you the Jerry to my Tom?" I spoke again, feeling nervous as I waited for a response.

"You think this is a game?" There was a lilt to his voice that I hadn't heard before and I shook my head slowly.

"I don't think this is a game."

"What is it you want from me, Lola?" He touched the side of my face softly.

"What is it I want from you? You're the one that—"

"You were going to leave without saying goodbye?" He frowned and stared at the bag in my hand. His voice was accusing as he stared into my eyes. "You were just going to fuck me and leave me?"

"Xavier." I blushed at the crudeness of his words.

"Yes?"

"That's not what was happening." I frowned and sighed. "Look, I don't want to do this anymore." I bit my lower lip. "What you said yesterday, you were right. I don't want to be in this world. I don't want to play these games. I don't want to be used or feel like I'm a pawn in a game you're playing with your friends and family."

"You think I've been using you as a pawn?" He was angry now, and I swallowed hard.

"I don't know," I said softly. "I just don't know anymore. I guess we can talk–"

"Enough!" His voice was loud and abrupt. "I'm done talking."

"So what do we do now?" I took a step back and felt the door behind me.

"What do you think?" He took a step toward me and I felt his hardness against my stomach as he leaned into me, his face hovering above mine.

"I don't know, that's why I'm asking," I said childishly, and his eyes narrowed again. His green eyes surveyed me in annoyance and I found it hard to look away from their sparkling brilliance.

"Now you receive your punishment." He grabbed my wrists and pulled them above my head and back against the door.

"My punishment?" I swallowed hard and he grabbed my bag from my hand and dropped it onto the ground. "Punishment for what?"

"Trying to leave." He growled again and I felt his tongue on my neck as his hands slid down the side of my body, stopping at my waist and working their way back up again.

"You're going to give me a punishment for trying to leave?" I licked my lips as his hands caressed the curve of my breasts.

"Don't you think you deserve one?" His fingers pinched my nipples and I moaned. Xavier smiled at the sound and leaned down and whispered in my ear.

"Are you ready?" His tone was soft and his breath tickled my inner ear. I moved against him slightly and he held my body more firmly against the door.

"Ready for my punishment?" I whispered, my mind filling with ideas of what he had planned. What would his punishment be? My legs tingled as I thought of all the things he might do to me. I groaned as I realized that I was turned on by the thought of doing some kinky-ass shit with Xavier. All thoughts of leaving right away had fled from my mind.

"Yes, your punishment."

"Punishment for leaving?" I gazed into his eyes, challenging him. "I can't leave? Is this a prison? Am I your prisoner? Am I your sex slave, Xavier?"

"What do you think, Lola?" His lips pressed against mine and he kissed me hard.

I stood there, still as a statue, doing everything in my power to stop myself from kissing him. He pulled away from me after a few seconds, looking annoyed that I hadn't kissed him back.

"What are you going to do to me?" I whispered, my mind imagining myself laid out on his bed with my ass in the air as he spanked me. I stifled another groan as I realized that would be a punishment I might be quite fond of.

"I think that's for me to know..." He grabbed my arms and pulled me against him tight. His arms wrapped around my waist and I felt my breasts crushed against his chest and I could feel his cock wiggling against my stomach.

"Xavier." I swallowed. "What are you doing?"

"Lola, that's my question for you. What is it that you think you're doing? Do you think I'm just going to let you walk out of here?" He stepped back from me suddenly and I felt bereft without his warm touch next to me.

"I just thought it would be better if I left before you woke up."

"Better in what way?" He shook his head. "Do you think that the guard wouldn't call me as soon as you walked downstairs? Did you really think you could just leave and never see me again?" His eyes searched my face. "And more importantly, is that what you wanted?"

"I...Xavier...I…" My voice croaked as I stared at him in confusion.

"I love you, Lola. I love you." He grabbed my face and kissed me softly. "Don't you understand that that's why I don't want you to leave? Don't you understand that that's why I need you to be with me?"

"You love me?" I said in shock and shook my head. "You're just saying that."

"I never just say anything." He shook his head. "I love you and I'm going to show you exactly what that means. I'm going to show you exactly what it means to be mine."

"What are you going to do to me, Xavier?" I said anxiously, my knees weakening at his words. He pulled me back away from the door and toward the bed, and I watched as he pulled out some candles from a drawer and lit them and placed them around the room. And then suddenly, I could hear the sounds of jazz playing from hidden speakers in the corners of the room.

"Xavier, what are you going to do?" I gasped, wondering what was going to happen next.

"What am I not going to do?" He grabbed my wrists and spun me around. "I'm going to show every inch of you exactly who I am and why I do what I do. I'm going to make every fiber of your body wonder where I've been all of your life. And I'm going to show you through words and actions just how much I love you."

"You can try to do that, I suppose," I said flippantly, my stomach churning in excitement. I could hardly believe that this moment was real. It was something I'd never expected to happen.

"Oh, I'm going to do more than try." His voice dropped. "I'm Xavier Van Romerius. I'm the Crown Prince of Romerius and I'm going to make sure that you never forget that."

"Or what?" I said softly, my heart racing as I saw the handcuffs suddenly appear in his hands.

"You'll just have to wait and see." His green eyes danced as he placed one of the metal cuffs over my right wrist. My breath caught as his eyes darkened and he leaned forward to whisper in my ear. " "No one leaves me, Lola, no one. You were going to try to leave earlier, but I'm glad that I woke up before you left. I'm going to show you exactly what a prince does to his lady-love, in the privacy of his room."

"I didn't leave." I swallowed hard. "You caught me before I left."

"And?" His eyes darkened.

"Is this..." I stumbled on the words as I spoke. I didn't know how to ask him if this was about love or sex. Did he really love me or did he just want my body? Was I just a possession to him?

"Is there something you want to ask me, Lola?" Xavier pushed me back onto the bed and sat down. His naked tanned chest teased me with its sexiness and I swallowed hard as I stared up at him.

"No, why would you think I wanted to ask you something?"

"I sense your emotions. I sense how you feel." And then he laughed. "And you were just about to ask me something. What are you feeling, Lola?"

"I'm not feeling anything," I lied.

"I want to tell you something. I need to tell you that there is no such thing as true love, Lola. People come and go from your life. You can't count on anyone being true to you, other than you." His eyes burned into mine. "So you must always speak your mind and live for the here and now. You never know what will happen in life."

"That's sad that you feel that way, Xavier." I spoke softly, my heart breaking at his words. "I believe in true love. I believe in one person loving another so much that they won't let anything get in their way." I licked my lips as he lay down next to me. "So what, then, do your words of love mean? Do you love me for me, or do you just want something from me?"

"Don't be a fool. Look around you, Lola. Everyone wants something. No one does anything just to be nice. No one loves someone for no reason at all."

"I do," I said, my heart breaking as I gazed at him. "I love you simply because you are you."

He stared at me then, his green eyes darkening at the look on my face. I could tell that I'd unnerved him. I could tell that that wasn't the response he'd wanted or expected to hear.

"I'm not good enough for you, Lola. I can't give you what you need and deserve." His voice broke as he spoke. "The path I'm on isn't for someone like you. I wish that it wasn't true, but it is. I do not deserve you." He jumped off of the bed and looked at me in anguish.

"What path is that?"

"The path of absolution." His gaze darkened. "The path of change."

"Who do you want to change?"

"I want to change the roles royals play in Europe. I want to create a new history."

"You think you can change the royal families of Europe?" I gazed at him, somewhat confused at what this had to do with his loving me and not believing in happily ever after.

"I have to change them," he said softly. "It's a dark history we have. If I could tell you stories of truth, if I could tell you things that people have done in the name of power…if I could tell you, then you would understand."

"What things, Xavier?"

"Rapes, murders, slavery." He leaned forward. "Casper's line has a history of evil."

"Isn't Casper's family related to yours, though?" I frowned.

"Not by blood." He shook his head and his eyes darkened with anger as he thought of his cousin. "I hate him for what he tried to do to you. When he had you in that room, Lola, I was so scared. I thought he was going to do something bad, something horrible. Something that would have made me kill him."

"What did you think he was going to do?"

"I don't want to talk about it." He shook his head. "It isn't something I want you to think about."

"Did you think he was going to rape me? Or did you think I would assent to his advances?" My voice was soft. "And which one would have been worse to you?"

Xavier glowered at me and ignored my question as he continued talking. "He wants to initiate Tarquin into his world and into the parties."

"I thought only the oldest brothers could attend those parties?"

"Casper makes the rules. He can change them as he pleases."

"What does he want to initiate Tarquin into?"

"The Society of Brothers," Xavier said and rubbed his forehead. He grimaced as he looked at me. "I shouldn't be telling you any of this."

"I'm glad you're telling me," I said softly. "Do you really love me, Xavier?"

"I do." He nodded and groaned. "I'm a fool, but I do."

"Do you trust me?" I said slowly, my eyes not leaving his.

"I do." He nodded again and my heart flipped over as he sat on the bed again and grabbed my hand. "I trust you with my heart."

"Then tell me what you want to do. Tell me how you want to make this change," I said softly. "Let me be a part of this."

"We'll have to go to another party. A grander ball. A darker ball. You'll be introduced to a world of games and glitter." His eyes glanced down at me. "I don't know..." His voice trailed off.

"I want to do this, Xavier. I want to be a part of this."

"Okay," he said, and suddenly he smiled as he leaned down to kiss me. "I was hoping you would say that." And then I kissed him back, and all thoughts of leaving were vanquished from my mind. All thoughts of leaving and going back to London without him were gone. I didn't want to be without Xavier. He was the Prince Charming I'd been looking for. Granted, he wasn't the Prince Charming of fairytales, but he was mine and he loved me. That was good enough for me. It was better than good enough. I was going to show Xavier that I could live in his world. I was going to show him that true love could last forever. I was going to show him that there was such a thing as happily ever after, even if I hadn't truly believed it until this very moment.

CHAPTER SIX
LOLA

There's a magical moment that occurs when two people who like each other stare at each other. There's a spark of electricity that seems to flow between just the two of them, and it doesn't matter how many other people are there. That moment is between just the two of them. That's how I felt when Xavier and I entered the grand entrance of the Royal Palace. He grabbed my hand, squeezed it tightly, and looked into my eyes with a deep, penetrating stare.

"It's all a game. If you remember that it's a game, then everything will be okay."

Xavier's voice was low as we walked into the palace.

"It's hard to think of it as a game," I said, taking a deep breath and hoping that the fresh air would provide me with the courage that I felt I was lacking.

"It's hard, but that is what this is, Lola." He stopped and looked toward me, his eyes scanning my face carefully. His green irises glowed like the gentle blades of grass in the morning as the sun was rising. They were gentle yet powerful in their beauty and elegance, warm and stoic all at the same time. "If you want to leave, just let me know." He squared his shoulders and I could see doubt in his eyes for a split second. "Maybe this isn't a good idea."

"No, we have to do this." I shook my head. "I can do this. I'm strong, Xavier. Stronger than you think."

"I know." He nodded. "You have to be strong to have stuck with me through all of this."

"You're a complex man." I laughed, suddenly feeling light inside.

"I think you're the only one that has ever truly seen me for who I am." His eyes pierced into mine and he just stared at me for a few seconds. "You've seen beyond my exterior, beyond my being a prince, beyond my abrasiveness. You've seen me for who I am and I still can't quite believe that you're here."

"You and me both." I laughed and he leaned forward and caressed my lips gently. His thumb brushed against my lower lip and moved gently back and forth.

"If ever there was a rose as beautiful as you, I'd plant it in my garden for when my days were blue. And I'd sit there and watch it, all the days through. Because that rose in my garden—well, it would remind me of you."

"I always knew you were a romantic, Xavier van Romerius." I smiled at him as my heart thudded at his words.

"That's good that you've thought so highly of me." He winked at me and then stilled, his face becoming serious once again. "Tonight, though, there will not be any romance. Tonight is not about romance. Tonight you will witness me as a man that I don't want to be. Tonight you will be introduced to a world that I didn't want to show you."

"It's okay, Xavier." I touched his shoulder. "I can handle it." I smiled at him, but my stomach was churning in fear and worry. To be honest, I wasn't really sure if I was going to be able to handle it. I wasn't sure what I was getting myself into. I wasn't sure what I was going to see. What was Xavier going to do? And would I be able to forgive him or myself if it crossed the mark? I loved this man and all of his flaws. I knew that he wasn't perfect. He was human, and had secrets that would make stronger women than me flee. But that was the beauty of love. It made us stronger. It gave us hearts of steel and guts of iron. I had a shield around me that could withstand a war for this man. I had a passion that could overcome mountains. My love for Xavier burned in my soul and ran through my veins, and I was willing to take this chance. I needed to show him that I could be there for him. And I also wanted a role in bringing Violeta and Casper down, after everything that they had done to ruin Xavier's name and to bring him down. I just couldn't let this happen to him again. I couldn't let them try to destroy the man I loved. The man who had stolen my heart the very first night we'd met.

"Let's do this." I licked my lips nervously and inhaled and exhaled a few times. "I'm ready."

"Just let me know if you're uncomfortable."

"I will." I nodded.

"This will be not be what you're expecting…" His voice trailed off and he looked nervous.

"How do you know what I'm expecting?"

"I didn't tell you everything." He closed his eyes. "Look Lola, there's—"

"Xavier. Lola." Casper's voice boomed as he interrupted Xavier and walked toward us. "I'm surprised to see you both here."

"Why?" I offered him a superior smile and tried to hide my distaste as I gazed at his handsome face. How could someone who looked so handsome and pure be as disgusting as he was? I didn't understand how my body could warm as I stared into his blue eyes, even when I knew how undeniably evil and callous he was.

"I'm glad that you're both here." He kissed both of my cheeks and pulled away. "It's always good to see you, Lola. So beautiful and pure, like a breath of fresh air."

"I wish I could say the same," I muttered as I glared at him. I was already feeling uncomfortable and I hoped this would be the first and last that I'd see of Casper tonight.

"Casper, there you are." Violeta appeared out of nowhere and walked up to us with an angelic smile on her beautiful face.

"Violeta." Xavier nodded and I scowled at the woman who had tried to make me leave Xavier with a lie.

"Darling, you look even more handsome than the last time we were here," Violeta said sweetly and stepped her right leg forward so that we could see the long expanse of her naked leg through the high slit in her silky midnight-blue dress.

"Is that possible?" Xavier raised an eyebrow at her.

"I didn't think so." Violeta reached over and brushed something off of his jacket, her perfectly manicured fingernails tapping against his chest lightly. "But then I've been known to be wrong."

"We all make mistakes." Xavier nodded and I was fuming. Did he seriously think that Violeta had made a mistake by saying that he was the father of the baby she'd given up? How could he be so chummy with her already? It infuriated me that this bitch was being treated with anything other than scorn.

"But everything comes right in the end," Casper said with a smirk on his face. "I am surprised to see you here, Xavier, but quite pleased."

"I'm sure you are."

"May the best man win," Casper said as he bowed his head and then looked at me. "To the victor go the spoils."

"You know, there is a painting by Rembrandt called *Night Watch*," Xavier said softly and deliberately as he held my hand.

"And?" Casper looked bored.

"It's called *Night Watch* because it depicts a city guard moving his troops out of the city," Xavier said and paused, smiling at everyone as he spoke. It was almost like he was in class again and talking about paintings to his students.

"Sounds boring." Casper yawned, but his eyes narrowed as he waited for Xavier to continue.

"The painting was covered with a dark varnish and that is why it had been called *Night Watch*," Xavier continued. "However, that varnish was removed and art collectors realized that the scene wasn't depicted at night at all." Xavier smiled. "So what was once seen as a guard leaving a city at night with his tail between his legs was really not accurate. The fact of the matter is that *Night Watch* wasn't a night watch at all." He looked at me then and I felt as if his words were directed at me only. "What we think we know and see is not always correct. And the winner isn't always the one that speaks the loudest or the most aggressively."

"I understand." I nodded at him and I could see Violeta frowning bitterly.

"Nice educational fable," Casper said and chuckled. "It's a pity that life isn't as simplistic as pictures, isn't it?"

"Paintings." Xavier frowned.

"Whatever." Casper shrugged and grabbed Violeta's hand. "Let's go back inside. The event is about to start."

"Let us go." She nodded and squared her shoulders back. "I'm ready."

"Good luck, my brother." Casper nodded at Xavier. "Here's to another successful Society of Brothers event."

"Yes, here's to another successful event," Xavier said, and I watched as Casper and

Violeta went back inside. I turned to Xavier and gazed at his face with a question.

"What's going on here, Xavier?" I touched his shoulder. "I don't understand what's going on."

"To be a leader, one must have control." His voice was tight. "One must have control and command over everything."

"What does that mean?"

"We can't talk now." He shook his head. "We need to go inside. Come, we can't miss the beginning." He grabbed my hand and escorted me down the hallways into a huge ballroom. I gasped at the crystal chandeliers hanging in the middle of the elegant room. There were about forty other couples there. The men were all dressed in tuxedos and the women were all in ball gowns. Each ball gown looked sexier than the last one and I no longer felt self-conscious in my skin-tight black gown, with the wide V-neck at the chest. The V was so low that the tops and sides of my breasts were exposed and pushed up. The material covering my nipples felt flimsy, and I'd been uncomfortable leaving the palace with Xavier in the dress, but now I felt conservative. Breasts seemed to be on display everywhere. Many of the dresses were so flimsy that they did nothing to cover the assets of most of the women in the room. I stood there feeling awkward as I looked around, and was about to say something to Xavier when the lights dimmed.

"Welcome, everyone," a tall, dark-haired man said from the front of the room. His voice was heavily accented and charismatic, and I stared at him in wonder. Who was this man who seemed to command the attention of everyone in the room?

"Who is that?" I asked Xavier curiously and he smiled at my dazed expression.

"Prince Stephan of Germany."

"Germany?" I said, surprised. "Really?"

"Not everyone in Germany is blond," Xavier said with a smirk.

"That wasn't why I was surprised. I didn't even know they had a royal family." I explained.

"Aww, I see. That's not surprising. You're American."

"You say that so patronizingly." I glared at him.

"Don't be sensitive." He grinned. "Now pay attention. Stephan's talk isn't to be missed." His eyes narrowed and he looked back to the front of the room.

"Whatever." I turned away from him and stared at the German prince on the stage in front of me. He was handsome—more handsome than Casper with his deceiving boyish good looks, and more roguish than Xavier. He looked like a Hollywood hunk, a rebel, a man who could command attention from everyone he encountered.

"I'm so glad that everyone could join us this weekend." He looked out at the crowd with a wide, genuine smile. His blue eyes were dazzling, and for a second his eyes met mine and he smiled, a wide welcoming smile, and I responded back automatically. In that moment I felt like we were the only two people in the room and my breath was taken away. "It brings me joy to see so many beautiful women in the room," he said, his eyes never leaving mine, and I felt myself blushing.

"I see my dear Lola isn't turned off by flattery," Xavier said in a dry voice, and I looked over at him. He had a wry smile on his face, but his eyes were anything but humored.

"He didn't say anything specifically to me," I said hurriedly, embarrassed at how easily I'd given myself away. Yes, I loved Xavier, but I wasn't immune to attention from a hot man.

"You're right." Xavier nodded. "His comment was directed to me and not to you."

"To you?" I frowned in confusion.

"It was a challenge." His eyes looked thoughtful.

"A challenge?"

"Do you know who runs the world?" Xavier asked me, his eyes serious.

"The presidents of the Western world?"

"No." He had a wry smile on his face. "They are figureheads. Interchangeable. They mean nothing. *We* run the world. The men in this room run the world."

"Oh." I waited for him to continue, as I wasn't quite sure what he was saying.

"And do you know what runs the world?" he whispered as Stephan continued to talk at the front of the room.

"No, what?" I shook my head.

"It's not money. It's not power. It's not sex. There is no power of the pussy." He grinned and then looked down toward my crotch. "Though pussy has a lot of power."

"Xavier!" I blushed.

"What runs the world, you ask?" he continued. "What runs the world is fearlessness. He who dares will always win. He who has no fear. He who can conquer and lead in any battle will always be on top."

"Battle?" I frowned.

"Battles don't mean war. Battles don't mean games. The most dangerous battles are the ones that happen behind closed doors. The ones that the everyday public don't see."

"I don't really know what you're talking about," I said with a whisper.

"The Society of Brothers is made up of royalty from all over the world. We have Arab sheikhs, African tribesmen, and British lords—anyone who is anyone. And we only have one leader and we have an inner circle. To make it into the inner circle one must completely trust their allies. When you control the world, nothing and no one can be more important than your trust in your fellow brothers."

"But you don't trust Casper, do you?"

"I need to make it into the inner circle." His eyes sought mine. "That is why we are here."

"What do you have to do to get into the inner circle?"

"I have to pass the test." He looked away from me. "It's all a game, Lola. It's a game to test my resolve. My patience. My power. My ability to assume authority."

"So how do they test it? What's the game?"

"You're a part of the game." His eyes burned into mine intensely. "They are going to test me by using you."

"Using me?"

"We're surrounded by beauty and riches. Money means nothing to anyone here. The most prized possession we all have is the woman by our side."

"You mean I'm your most prized possession?" I grinned. "And by the way, I'm not your possession, but I'm going to ignore that for now."

"This isn't a joking matter, Lola." His face looked grave. "These men, these men are powerful and calculated. They will say and do anything."

"You mean like Violeta?" I asked softly. "She's not a man, though."

"Everyone here is capable of things you wouldn't want to tell your children at night."

"What are they going to do to me?"

"That's completely up to you," he said, and then turned away and started applauding with the rest of the crowd as Stephan had stopped speaking. "I'm going to go and get us some wine, okay?"

"Okay." I nodded, but I didn't really want him to go. I wanted him to explain to me what he was talking about. I wanted to know what these men wanted of me or from me. I stood there for a few seconds just studying my hands. I could barely believe that I was in this situation. It was surreal and also exhilarating.

"Hello." A deep sensual voice spoke from in front of me and I looked up. It was Prince Stephan, and his blue eyes looked warm and inviting.

"Hello," I said almost shyly as I stood there. Why had he come up to talk to me? I looked to see if Xavier was close by, but he had disappeared into the crowd.

"Can I show you around?"

"Around?"

"My palace." He smiled and placed his hand in front of me. "I can show you the rooms that no one else gets to see."

"I shouldn't. I'm waiting on someone."

"It won't take long." He cocked his head. "I think you'll find it quite exciting."

"I... I guess, sure," I said and bit my lower lip as I immediately regretted agreeing to go with this man I'd just met.

"Good." He smiled and his hand was warm and soft as it grazed my arm. "Let me show you around. I like to make sure all my guests are well taken care of." His eyes fell to my breasts and he licked his lips slightly as he looked back into my face. My heart skipped a beat at the expression of lust in his eyes. I followed behind him like a lamb, not sure what I was doing, but feeling like I was being led to my slaughter.

CHAPTER SEVEN
XAVIER

I heard a couple of the local girls whispering and giggling behind me as I waited to collect the two glasses of wine. One of them was a bit more confident than the rest and she whispered a little bit louder, hoping I would hear her and turn around. I knew the deal and I wasn't interested. I didn't have any interest in checking out any of their goods. I didn't have time for a fling. Not this time. And I didn't want one, either. The only woman I wanted was Lola. Though I knew they didn't care about that. In fact, they would see it as an even bigger challenge. Sleeping with a prince was one thing, but sleeping with a prince who was in love with another sweetened the deal to these women. It was another part of my world that I found distasteful.

"He's so dreamy," one of the girls sighed to her friend, and I hid a smile as I looked back and made eye contact with the girl: a cute redhead. If she only knew the truth. I was anything but dreamy. I turned back around and frowned to myself as I realized that I'd lost sight of Lola. I'd allowed myself to get distracted at the wrong time. I didn't know where she was. Who was after her? Who would be the first one to test her? I wanted to slam my fist against the wall. The games had started and already they had the upper hand. I looked around the room quickly to see if I could find her, but she was nowhere to be seen. And then I saw Stephan, hurrying up the stairs with a smile on his face, and I knew. It had started. And suddenly I was afraid. I was afraid that I was going to lose, and in that moment I wished that I'd never brought Lola here with me.

CHAPTER EIGHT
LOLA

Heart beating fast. Check.

Temperature rising. Check.

Sexy man in front of me. Check.

Mind racing in fear. Check.

And then he said my name: slowly, deeply, softly, enjoying the taste of it as it slipped from his lips.

"Lola." He said my name again and I froze.

This prince—this stranger—knew my name. I knew his name was Stephan because he'd been speaking to everyone at the front of the room. He was obviously the man of the night. He'd not been introduced to me, though. We'd not even been in the same vicinity until this moment. He hadn't even glanced at me, except for that one moment when he was speaking. That one moment that Xavier had said was a direct challenge to him. I shivered in the cool room. My resolve was leaving me. I wasn't sure that I was ready for this game that had seemed so easy when arriving at the palace. Xavier had tried to warn me that it wouldn't be easy. That this was a dark world. I hadn't realized what he meant, but now I did. It wasn't just dark because of the people I was with. It was dark because of my feelings as well. Stephan smiled at me, his eyes looking at my lips for a few seconds before looking back into my eyes.

"Lola is such a beautiful name," he said in his beautiful, melodic voice, his German accent somehow sounding more sexy than guttural.

I froze as I stared at him, wondering what was going to happen next. Who was this man? I'd never met him before this night, but he knew my name and his eyes were staring into mine with a fiery, passionate look. I swallowed hard as I wondered what he knew, how he knew, if he knew everything that was going on. Even more worrying to me was the wonder of what he wanted. I took a step back, wanting to leave, and then he grabbed me around the waist and pulled me toward him.

"Kiss me," he commanded, and this time his words were hard and impatient. I shivered as I felt his body pressed against mine intimately. He was turned on and that made me happy and powerful, for some inexplicable reason. I closed my eyes and leaned forward, ready to taste him, wanting to know who he was, but then I pulled back, my brain overcoming the shroud of lust that filled me every time I gazed at him. He was too handsome for his own good. Too sexy. He had too much charm and I shook my head slightly, feeling embarrassed that I'd gotten caught up in the moment so easily.

"How do you know my name?" I stared up at him with wide eyes. And I knew my expression showed my surprise when he chuckled.

"What don't I know about you, Lola?" His eyes darkened for a second before he leaned down and kissed me softly. His lips tasted like salted cherries and I was unprepared for the shock that ran through me as his tongue entered my mouth, smooth and steady. I reached up and grabbed his neck to stop from falling to the ground as my legs started shaking. His eyes laughed into mine as he continued kissing me. I didn't kiss him back, but I wasn't able to stop him. In that moment I couldn't think or act or do anything. I didn't care who he was or what he wanted. All I could think about was the fact that his lips were on mine and burning a deep desire down into my soul, and then he pulled away. I groaned involuntarily and he laughed as he studied my red face.

"I want to know everything about you, Lola." His fingers traced a line down my face as he stared at me intently. "I'm not going to let you leave until I know everything."

And that's when the ground beneath me felt like it was shaking, like some sort of earthquake had hit. Suddenly, I was afraid and totally aware of my environment. I wanted to cry out in shame as I realized what I'd just done and felt. I'd let him kiss me, intimately. And for a split second I'd enjoyed it. For a split second his intensity had overwhelmed me. And that is when my body started trembling uncontrollably. Suddenly, it struck me that this man might be the one person that Xavier had been trying to warn me about. Maybe Prince Stephan was the one I should have been worried about. Maybe Casper was nothing but an innocent distraction. Maybe Stephan was the top dog. Maybe that was why Casper and Violeta had not stopped Xavier from attending tonight. Maybe they were nothing but pawns to be ignored and discarded.

"Tell me your deepest desire and I'll create your darkest fantasy," Stephan said, and I didn't know how to respond. I didn't want to respond, but my imagination was running wild. Was he propositioning me?

"Wh-What are you talking about?" I stuttered, my eyes wide. I didn't anticipate his swift reply or how quickly he would pull me into his arms again.

"Spend one week with me. Let me pleasure you and show you how I can make your fantasies come to life." His blue eyes looked dark with desire as he stared at me with such intensity that I wouldn't have been surprised if bolts of fire had emanated from him. All of a sudden I was taken back to what Casper had said to me in the room in Delmar when he tried to convince me to have a threesome. Hadn't he said something similar? Hadn't he also wanted to take me on a sexual journey? And then I realized that this was the game. They were trying to get me. I was the prize. Or rather, I wasn't the prize, but the goal. Whoever ended up with me was the winner, even though I wasn't important to Casper or Stephan. They were trying to usurp Xavier. Xavier had brought me here for a reason. He trusted me. He trusted that I could play the game and not fall under Casper or Stephan's spell. Unlike Violeta. Violeta had fallen for Casper and then gotten pregnant. Only she had been discarded by all of them because Xavier had never really cared for her. Not like he cared for me. He'd been right. This world was dark and scary. And I wasn't sure that I was prepared to play the game. I was attracted to Stephan in a way I hadn't been attracted to Casper. It was easy for me to say no to Casper, but I knew it would be harder with Stephan, even though I didn't want him mentally. There was just something about him physically that drew me in and mesmerized me. Something that made time stand still and made me forget exactly who I was and what I was doing. And that scared me. I'd never been so inexplicably drawn to a man. Not even Xavier, though I'd thought of him as a sex god the first time I'd seen him.

"What do I have to do during that week?" I asked softly, my voice a whisper as I answered him. I couldn't believe we were having this conversation. Or rather, I couldn't believe that I was having this conversation with him. I couldn't believe I was playing this game, letting him think that I was actually entertaining the idea of spending a week with him.

"Submit." He growled as he leaned toward me. "All you have to do is submit." He grabbed my wrists and pulled them up above my head. My heart beat fast as his fingers dug into my skin. I could feel my chest rising and I watched him staring at the exposed parts of my breasts.

I swallowed hard as I stared at his handsome, brooding face, and I knew exactly what my answer was going to be. I knew exactly what my answer had to be if I wanted to find out all of his secrets and how far this game was going to go. I wished that I could speak to Xavier. I wished that I could find out what he wanted from me. "So what do you say, Lola?" He dropped my hands and stepped back. "Will you spend the next seven nights with me?"

I nodded slowly and I watched as a wide smile spread across his face. He looked away as a flash of excitement and power invaded his soul. I looked down and tried to hide my smile. I had him where I wanted him. Prince Stephan actually believed that this was the beginning of his wicked week with me. He actually believed that he was going to succeed where Casper had failed. He believed that I was going to capitulate to him and forget Xavier. He believed that his sex appeal meant more to me than my love for Xavier. He had no idea that I had other plans. He had no idea that he was the one who was going to get played. I just hoped that whatever games Xavier had planned wouldn't extend past the night. I knew that Xavier had to have known that I would be tested. And I knew that he had faith in me. I was going to play along for now. I was going to see what happened next.

"Let's leave now, then," he said abruptly, and my heart stopped. This was not what I'd expected. There was no way I was going to leave with him *now*. This was not what was supposed to happen next. All of a sudden I felt like a little kid, and panic and anxiety filled me. I wished more than ever that Anna were here with me.

"I'm here with someone. I can't just leave now." It was true. He knew I was here with Xavier.

"That someone is not a threat to me." He smiled and I stared at his perfect white teeth. This man was gorgeous and fearless, and my heart thudded as he looked me over admiringly.

"A threat?" I frowned. What did he mean by that?

"I'm not worried about any other men in your life."

"Excuse me? There are not multiple other men in my life." I bit my lower lip as he leaned closer to me. Was he going to kiss me again? I knew that he was an asshole and that I couldn't let him kiss me again. I could see in his eyes that he just wanted to have sex with me. I didn't like his assumption that he could just kiss me again as he pleased, and I was worried that he might try to do something else.

"That's why I said I'm not worried about any other men." He stopped moving when his lips were a mere inch away from mine. I could feel his breath on my face and my lips trembled slightly at his proximity. "Xavier is not a threat to me."

"Stephan, no," I said, annoyed as he made to kiss me again. I didn't want him to have the upper hand already. I was already failing Xavier by allowing him to kiss me and lose my head.

"No?"

"That's what I said," I snapped.

"Feisty. I like that." He grinned at me and I watched as he ran his hands through his dark, silky hair. He looked at me thoughtfully. "You're different from the others."

"The others?" I took a step back from him and frowned. How many others had there been?

"They don't matter." He shook his head. "I want you to do me a favor."

"A favor? How?" I ran my hands down my side, wondering what he was going to ask me.

"Dance with me."

"Dance with you?" I said in surprise.

"Yes, unless your boyfriend would have a problem with it."

"He's my fiancé and he would have a huge problem with it."

"We both know he's not really your fiancé." Stephan scoffed. "Why did he leave—"

"Lola, there you are." Xavier pushed open the door. "I've been looking for you." He strode into the room, worry on his face, and he looked at my red face with a disapproving look.

"Hello, Xavier." Stephan smiled at Xavier wildly and then looked at me. "Like I said, he's not a threat. Lola, shall we leave now?" He chuckled and I could feel my face burning with shame and embarrassment. I avoided his gaze and looked at Xavier, who was scowling. I had no idea why he'd come up here or what he expected from me. My heart beat with love as I looked at his face. He looked jealous, worried and concerned and I could see the love in his eyes as he stared at me. It was hard to believe that he loved me too. He was too handsome and too rich to be interested in someone like me. I felt confused and out of my comfort zone with all these handsome princes trying to woo me and bed me. Men like them didn't approach me, and I was glad for it now. I was glad that I hadn't had to deal with situations like these all my life. I wouldn't have known how to handle dating men like these when I was younger. Not that I thought that Stephan wanted to date me. Oh no. I knew from the look in his eyes that dating was the last thing he wanted to do. He wanted to take me to bed. Or rather, he wanted to fuck me. I looked at Stephan and the primal look on his face, and I knew 'fuck' was the operative word. He was not a man who made love. He didn't want to kiss and caress me and ensure that I had an orgasm every single time. He wanted to fuck me. Hard and deep. And take what he wanted. He wanted to dominate in every sense of the word. And a part of me—a part

I didn't even know existed—was secretly thrilled by that fact. A part of me wondered what it would be like to be taken wildly and with abandon. I stared at Xavier then and I knew that I was going to tell him my thoughts. I was going to tell him that I wanted to explore and experiment. I wanted to be taken on a journey of desire, as Stephan had said. Only I didn't want Stephan to be the one taking me there. I wanted it to be Xavier.

"Shall we leave, Lola?" Stephan said again. "Are your lips aching to be kissed by mine once more?"

I looked down in shame as Xavier glared at me, his eyes narrowing. "Lola's not going anywhere." Xavier's voice was harsh as he spoke to Stephan. "You, of all people, know how this works, Stephan."

"I know how it works," Stephan said lightly and then looked at me. "I just don't think that she knows or is prepared for what comes next."

"What comes next?" I asked, my eyes wide as I looked to Xavier's face. His expression was unreadable and I could tell that he was still angry with me. I wanted to explain to him that I hadn't wanted Stephan to kiss me. I wanted to explain to him that I'd been in a haze and that I loved him. There was no one I wanted more than him.

"Next is the Touch of a Kiss competition." Stephan's words sounded lyrical. "I wasn't going to subject you to it, but I think that Xavier has other plans."

"Xavier? What is the Touch of a Kiss competition?" My voice sounded shaky as I spoke to him.

"It's the first step of the games." Xavier's voice was bleak. "It's where you decide whose touch turns you on the most."

"What?" My eyes bulged as I gazed at him.   "What?"

"It's the first game to reach the inner circle." Xavier's eyes stared into mine. "And you won't be touched by any hands."

"What do you mean?" I said, frowning, not understanding.

"He means that Xavier's fate is in your hands, Lola." Stephan smiled and walked toward the door. "What you decide tonight will determine how far Xavier gets in the Society   of   Brothers."

"Xavier?" I asked him softly. "What is he talking about?"

"Tonight we find out if it is really me you want, or if you crave another." Xavier's eyes looked at my lips and he turned away from me and sighed. "We see if you pass the test."

"What is the test?"

"Let's go now, and you'll find out," Stephan said from his spot by the door. "Unless you want to back out now, Xavier?"

"No," Xavier said firmly as he looked back at me. "I want to know exactly who Lola wants and who she's going to choose." He looked at me again and then walked to the door. I followed behind both of them, my heart racing. I didn't know what was going to happen next and for some strange reason that didn't scare me. For once in my life, I was going to ride out the wave and let it take me where it wanted to. I didn't even feel guilty. Xavier was the one who had put me in this position. Xavier was the one who wanted us to continue. At this point, it was out of my hands. He'd taken me into his world and I was about to find out just how deep and dark it could get.

CHAPTER NINE
XAVIER

I could still see Lola's lipstick on Stephan's lips. Bright red and smudged. My blood was boiling and I was mad at Lola and myself for what had happened. I should have known that Stephan would want to take part this year. He always had something to prove. He always needed to be number one. He always had to prove that he was the man. He wanted to be the King of kings. The Prince of princes. The one we all looked up to. He wanted to prove that he was capable of taking over the society. He wanted to be in the inner circle as badly as I did. And I knew he was willing to do everything that he could to end up as the final winner. I'd known that Stephan would want it badly, but I hadn't thought he'd seen me as his biggest competition. I had known as soon as he'd focused on Lola, though, that I was the one to beat. I was the target. This wasn't between Casper and me. This was between Stephan and me. And that made me uncomfortable. I knew that Stephan had charms that Casper couldn't even dream about. And I knew that he had a way of luring women into his web. He was the pied piper of women and I needed to make sure that he didn't have Lola following behind him. I needed to make sure that I was the one she chose. Not only because that was what I needed to make it to the inner circle, but also because my heart would never be the same if she chose someone else.

CHAPTER TEN
LOLA

Xavier, Stephan and I walked in silence down the long corridor and down a flight of steps. The walls were adorned with paintings and as I looked at them I realized they were likely portraits of Stephan's ancestors.

"That's my great-great grandfather, Wilhelm, and next to him is his father, Frederick." Stephan smiled at me as he caught me staring at the paintings.

"They look so serious," I said simply and then paused. "Is there a reason why they all had those beards?"

"You don't like the unkempt look?" Stephan winked at me as he teased me and I could see Xavier tensing as he walked beside us.

"I've just never seen any royals look so..." I paused as I tried to find the way to voice my thoughts diplomatically.

"Common?" Stephan asked and his blue eyes laughed as I nodded, feeling embarrassed. I'd been about to say that they reminded me of hillbillies that I'd seen on *Duck Dynasty*, but I was glad I'd kept my mouth shut. He most probably didn't even know what *Duck Dynasty* was and it was likely that he and Xavier would just think I was some American hick; which, to be quite honest, I was. And proud to be. Kinda.

"Are you feeling okay, Lola?" Xavier abruptly changed the subject and looked at me.

"I'm fine." I nodded, but in reality I was far from fine. In reality I was over my head. "I don't suppose I can make a quick phone call, can I?"

"Phone call?" Xavier looked perplexed and I could understand why. This was neither the time nor place for me to be asking to make a call.

"Is there some sort of emergency?" Stephan looked concerned and it struck me that it was odd that he was the one who cared more about me or was at least acting like he did.

"No." I shook my head. "I'm just worried that my best friend, Anna, has wondered what happened to me as I haven't spoken to her in a while."

"Then you must call her now." Stephan stopped. "It will have to be quick because they are waiting for us in the main room downstairs."

"Oh, I don't have to call if people are waiting for us." I looked at Xavier then, to figure out what he wanted me to do.

"Call." His eyes pierced into mine and he nodded slightly. "Nothing is so important that you can't call your best friend to let her know you're okay."

"My, my, you must be a magic woman." Stephan grinned at me. "Nothing would have stopped Xavier last time he was in this position."

"Last time?" I said as my stomach dropped, though I already knew what Stephan was going to say.

"Yes, when he was here with Violeta." Stephan said her name distastefully. "Why, that was the most drama we'd ever had at one of these balls."

"Why was that?" I asked, not able to look at Xavier.

"It's not really my place to say." He looked at Xavier's scowling face. "I assume that it still hurts."

"Hurts?" Xavier looked amused. "No, it doesn't hurt."

"I suppose it's more a pride thing." Stephan nodded. "I know if my date fucked my cousin at an event I'd taken her to and let everyone watch, I'd be pretty sore myself."

"Violeta did what she had to do." Xavier shrugged. "I don't fault her."

"Hopefully it doesn't happen again this year," Stephan said casually. "That would really burn."

"I'm not worried." Xavier's voice was harsh and he leaned forward and grabbed Stephan's shirt and whispered harshly,

"There'd better be no game-playing with Lola. Everyone had better stick to the rules or heads are going to roll."

"I always stick to the rules." Stephan shook him off and smiled. "I'm not Casper. I don't need to break them."

"What rules? What are you guys talking about?"

"Xavier hasn't told you about the test?" Stephan sounded surprised, but I could tell by the look in his eyes that he was faking it. He was a good actor, though. I could almost believe that he cared about me and what I was going through. Almost, but not quite. The simple fact was that he had no reason to care about me. He didn't know me. The fact that he'd kissed me showed me that he was going full force. He was trying to woo me hard. I just didn't really understand why. Was this really just a macho thing?

"Test?" I glanced at Xavier and he pulled out his phone instead of answering me. "Call Anna and talk to her," he said. "Then come back and tell me if you want to stay."

"What's the test, Xavier?" I asked him, but he remained stoic.

"It's a test of passion and desire," Stephan said. "It's a test of lust and want."

"Oh?" My eyes searched Xavier's, but still he didn't speak.

"It's a test to see if Xavier is really the man to turn up your fires." Stephan's eyes burned into mine. "Or perhaps he was just the man you met first. Perhaps you are more suited to someone else. Perhaps your sexual journey will take a different turn." He licked his lips deliberately as he spoke and I turned away hurriedly and walked a few yards away to make my call. I listened to the phone ringing and ringing and I was so scared that Anna wasn't going to answer.

"Hello," she said sleepily and I almost fainted in relief because I was so happy to hear her voice.

"Anna, it's me, Lola."

"Lola," she almost screamed. "Where are you?"

"I'm in some palace in Germany, I think," I whispered into the phone. "I'm not sure what I've gotten myself into."

"What do you mean?"

"I mean, I think these rich people are freaks. They have sex games and sex clubs and women seem to be disposable to them."

"What are you talking about, Lola? Is Xavier there?"

"Yes and he's wonderful, Anna. He told me he loves me. He told me that he thinks that I'm the only woman he's ever loved."

"So why don't you sound happy?" Anna said softly. "Shouldn't you be jumping for joy now that you have your Prince Charming?"

"There's more," I sighed. "He doesn't believe in true, everlasting love and—well, there's someone else."

"Someone else? Not that guy, Casper?" Anna gasped. "Sebastian told me about him."

"No, not Casper." I peeked over my shoulder and saw that Xavier and Stephan were both staring at me.

"Did you see Sebastian, by the way?" Anna asked. "I think he was flying over today."

"No," I said quickly. "Look, Anna, I can't talk long, but I'm confused. I think I might be attracted to this other prince."

"Another one?"

"He's German and captivating and he kissed me and I hated it and loved it at the same time."

"I thought you loved Xavier?"

"I do," I breathed out, my heart racing just thinking about him. "I love him deeply, but there's something about Stephan that appeals to my primal side."

"You want to fuck him?" Anna said crudely and I blushed.

"No, of course not," I said quickly and honestly. However, that was only a partial truth. It was true that I didn't want to sleep with him, but a part of me that I hadn't known existed until tonight thought that it could be wild and exciting to just think about the possibilities of what could happen.

"So what's the problem, then?"

"I think I'm caught up in some sort of sexual maze and erotic mastery, Anna. I think I'm caught up in some sort of late night almost erotic kinky shit and it's scaring the hell out of me."

"What scares you the most?" she asked me softly and I sighed as I answered her.

"I'm scared by the fact that I'm as turned on as I am appalled. Does that make me a crazy person?"

"No." Her voice was warm. "That makes you human. That makes you real. That makes you as complicated and fucked up as everyone else on the planet. Listen to me, Lola. Think of this as your own personal sexual revolution. I know you're feeling guilty because you have the hots for another guy, even though you love Xavier. But Xavier has been an asshole to you in the past, Lola. If he truly loves you, then he'll have to understand whatever is going on."

"I'm scared, Anna. I wish you were here."

"I wish I was there as well. I want to meet the man that can tempt you away from Xavier."

"He's not tempting me away, Anna. He's just making it hard for me to think straight."

"Wet pantics will do that to you." Anna laughed and I groaned.

"I have to go," I said hurriedly. "Thank you for being you."

"Have a good time, Lola. Remember that if you feel uncomfortable at any point, just leave. If push comes to shove, call me collect and I'll get you a ticket so you can come back to London."

"Thank you, Anna," I said and hung up the phone. I took a deep breath and turned around and hurried back to the men. Both

Xavier and Stephan were looking at me as if I were the last woman on Earth and it made me feel a thrill of power and sexuality that I'd never wanted to own before.

***

We walked into a large room with couches on one side and a glass wall on the other side. There were four other men waiting in the room, including Casper, and three other women, including Violeta. I wasn't happy to see Violeta and Casper in the room standing there, looking nonchalant. I checked out the other faces in the room, but I didn't recognize any of them from the parties I'd attended with Xavier previously.

"Welcome, everyone. My name is Charles. I'm a member of the Dutch royal family and the inner circle of the Society of Brothers." The tall man with the long nose looked very pleased with himself and I couldn't help but stare at the smirk on his face. "I'll be the proctor today." He laughed. "I will go over the rules and placements and then we shall start."

"Are you feeling okay?" Xavier asked me quietly as we listened to Charles talking. "What did Anna say?"

"She said to stay as long as I feel comfortable." I made a face at him. "Honestly, I don't know if I'm okay and I don't know if I'm comfortable, but I want to do this for you. You want to make it to that inner circle, right?"

"I do." He nodded solemnly.

"Then let's get you there," I said and tried to ignore the feeling of warmth that had spread through my body as I'd noticed Stephan staring at me. "Let the games begin," I said under my breath and I closed my eyes for a few seconds to stop myself from staring back into Stephan's penetrating gaze. I had no idea what was going to happen next, but I knew I was more excited than I should have been, given the circumstances.

CHAPTER ELEVEN
XAVIER

All's fair in love and war they say. I don't know if I believe that anymore. I don't feel like I believe it. My stomach is in knots as I stare at Lola, her face a mask of worry and excitement. The worry I understand and, unfortunately, the excitement I do as well. I've seen the looks she's been exchanging with Stephan. The promises in his eyes. I could kill him for the looks he's giving her, but I know he's doing it to rile me up. He's doing it to make me lose focus. They don't want me in the inner circle. Casper and Stephan are threatened by the changes I would make. They don't want the status quo to be different. They don't want to lose their authority and power. And that's exactly why I want in so badly. I was mad at myself and at Lola's friend Anna for letting Lola go through with this. For me. She was doing it for me and I felt sick to my stomach. It was a means to an end, but I didn't wonder if I wasn't selling my soul to the devil to reach that end. She looked so beautiful standing there next to me, waiting. I could see all eyes on her, wondering who she was and what she had that she'd gotten me. I could see the snarl on Violeta's face as she glanced at Lola. She was going to make it even more uncomfortable for her, I just knew it. I was about to grab Lola's arm and whisk her out of the room. I was about to grab her and tell her—command her—to leave with me, but as I stood there, I realized that a part of me didn't want to. A part of me wanted to know who she was going to choose. A part of me didn't want to give up the power of waiting to see what was going to happen. I didn't know if that was stupid of me or not. I didn't know what I should be doing as a man who loved her. For I was almost positive that I loved her with every fiber of my being. It was only a little voice in the back of my head that made me doubt myself. It asked me why I would have even brought her here if I loved her. That was the voice I ignored. That was the voice I didn't want to hear. No one questioned my motives. Not even my subconscious.

CHAPTER TWELVE
LOLA

"Can I have everyone's attention, please?"

Charles spoke up loudly, his voice smug as he looked around the room. I could see the other two girls looking as timid as I felt, and Violeta stood there proud and comfortable.

"Can I have all the girls come up to me, please?" He waved us over to him and I looked at Xavier, my heart pounding. He gazed at me with a slightly anxious expression and I knew that he was wondering if I was going to go ahead.

"You don't have to do this," he said softly as he stepped towards me, his hands touching my waist lightly. "If you're not comfortable, we can leave."

"We don't have to leave." I shook my head. "I'm fine," I lied and watched the three other girls walking over to Charles. "I'm fine," I said again as I made my way over to Charles myself. My warm face told me I was a liar, as did my clammy hands. I was freaking out inside. I had no idea what was about to go on. I had no idea if I was going to be okay with what was about to go on. And even worse, I wasn't sure how I felt about heading into the unknown. A part of me felt excited and tingly all over. It wasn't an emotion I was used to: this heart-pounding, panty-wetting, fear-inducing excitement.

"I'm going to be in charge today and I want to explain what's going to happen," Charles said as he gazed at all four of us.

"Before we go into the main room, you can all wear as much or as little as you want."

"Do we have to take our clothes off?" the girl next me said and I looked at Charles for his answer. They didn't really expect us to take our clothes off, did they? They couldn't expect that. At least not yet.

"At this point, you can wear as little or as much as you want," he repeated, his eyes peering at the girl in such a way that let her know that as little as possible was preferred. I heard Violeta giggling as she unzipped her dress and stepped out of it. It fell to the ground and she lifted her long, tan legs up and moved to the side. I gazed at her body in admiration and a little bit of jealousy. She looked perfect in her slinky black thong—covering her pert ass—and her small black bra. I was envious of her sexy body. I felt like I didn't come close to matching up, at least next to her. Her stomach was toned as well and I felt my stomach dropping as I looked back at the men to see if they were staring at her. My face grew red as I felt Xavier's eyes on me. He had a small grin on his face as he raised an eyebrow at me and I knew that he'd watched me staring at Violeta. I raised an eyebrow back at him and he licked his lips and winked. For a few seconds I was taken back to that first meeting in the museum. It felt like years ago, even though it had only been months. My stomach still jumped at the sight of his silky black hair and laughing green eyes. He was so handsome, so suave, so sexy. He was a sex god personified and I swallowed hard thinking about being with him, having him next to me, filling me up, taking what he wanted.

"Are you ready, Lola?" Charles' voice snapped me out of my daydream and I nodded back in silence.

"Then let's go into the room. I'll explain the rules in further detail there," he said and opened a door. We all followed him into the room silently and I wondered if I had lost my mind. I looked around the room and the first thing I noticed was a big king-sized bed. Then I stepped back and looked around properly. The room was spacious and there was a huge window that appeared to be double-glazed. One of the girls saw me looking at it and made a face. I stared at her questioningly, not wanting to ask her why she looked so apprehensive, not wanting to know exactly what was going to go on today, in case it made me want to flee far away from here.

"They can see us." She nodded towards the window. "It's how they keep it fair."

"Keep what fair?" I replied, keeping my voice low. I could see Violeta staring at us with narrowed eyes, but I turned my back on her.

"The tests," the girl said and made another face. "Each round you accept, the stakes get higher and higher, but there are restrictions. The windows are there to keep the men honest."

"I see," I said in a small voice, though I had no idea what she was talking about.

"We can't see out, though," she continued. "We can't see anything. And they blow some sort of overpowering air freshener into the room, so you can't tell anything based on smell, either."

"Oh, wow." I looked at her consideringly. "How do you know all of this?"

"My sister came last year," she said and shrugged. "She told me, well, she was trying to warn me not to come."

"Oh?"

"She chose wrong." The girl bit her lower lip. "Her lover, Prince Marx, wasn't allowed entry to the inner circle and then he went and married Caroline, a lord's daughter from Belgium."

"Oh, no." My eyes widened. "That's awful."

"Yes." She nodded. "My sister lives with our parents with her son and she cries every night."

"Her son?" I asked, shocked. "Not Marx's son as well?"

"Yes, but he's a bastard so he doesn't count." She nodded, her voice matter-of-fact. "My sister told me that a part of her knew it wasn't Marx when Casper entered her."

"Casper?" My jaw dropped and then my face paled. "Did you say 'entered her'?"

"Yes." She nodded and then touched my hand. "Don't panic, that's the later rounds—"

"All right, ladies," Charles said, cutting the girl off and I stared at him with my heart in my mouth. Was another man going to try and have sex with me? Oh, my God, what had I agreed to do? "As most of you know, you're about to take part in a series of tests. These tests are in place for two reasons. Firstly, they are to prove that you know your lover better than anyone in the world. Secondly, they are to bond the princes of the world together. These bonds are unbreakable and only when a prince passes all of the tests of the inner circle will he be allowed to join."

"What does that mean?" the fourth girl asked, her voice soft. "I don't understand what we're doing here?"

"There will be four tests tonight," Charles said simply and he went to sit on the bed. He sat back and gazed at us. "They are all very simple, but with each round the stakes will be increased."

"What do you mean by tests?" I spoke up.

"Sex games," he said with a smile. "That's the easiest explanation."

"Sex games?"

"We need to choose our partner," the girl next to me said. "In each round, two men will do something to you, and you won't see who they are. You have to choose the one that gave you the most pleasure. If you choose your mate, you advance to the next round. If you go through all four rounds and choose your mate, he is allowed to enter the inner circle."

"Oh?" I bit my lower lip. "And they can do anything to you?"

"Yes." Violeta looked at me and smiled, a smug, bitchy smile.

"Well, not exactly," Charles corrected her. "Each round is different. Like this first round, neither of the men can use their hands or any other parts of their body to tease you."

"Okay." I let out my breath. "What's the point of this all, though?"

"A prince that wants to be part of the inner circle must have control over every part of his life. Once he reaches this point, he has proven to others that he is good in business and in controlling his country, but we all know that the biggest test of control is with our partner. If a prince can show that he has mastered what his partner craves and likes, then he can show that he has attention to detail that is so finite that he can control the world." Charles paused. "And, of course, we all know that the princes in the inner circle are the ones that rule the world."

"So they are trying to pleasure us?" I said and licked my lips nervously. "And we don't know who is touching us?"

"That is correct." Charles nodded.

"Wait, so the guys are all going to touch the other girls as well?" My voice caught as I grew jealous. Did that mean Xavier was going to be touching Violeta?

"They can choose to be a part of all of the tests or just the test of the woman they brought," Charles said. "All of the princes, aside from Xavier, chose to be with all the women."

"So Xavier is or isn't going to be with other women?" I asked again to make sure I clarified his answer.

"Xavier will only be in a room with you," he said, unblinking, as he looked at me. "You must be special."

"Oh, I don't know." My voice trailed off, but I smiled to myself. He wasn't going to be messing around with any other girls. He didn't want anyone else. Just me. It made me feel special. Inexplicitly special and I knew I was a fool. I had no idea what these other men were going to do to me. I had no idea how far this was going to go. "So what happens in round two?" I asked. "The same thing with different girls?"

"No." Charles smiled. "In round two, everyone that chooses to remain in the tests will be told of the new rules."

"You have to remove an article of clothing then," Violeta said and stared at my dress with narrowed eyes. "And they can use body parts, too."

"Well, no hands. Or cocks," Charles said.

"Yeah, not until later rounds," Violeta said and looked me in the eyes. "I hope you can tell Xavier's thrusts from another's. I'd hate for you to be fucked by another and choose him. Just imagine how hurt Xavier would be." My breath caught as I gazed at her and it wasn't because I was worried that I'd choose another man over Xavier. It was the fact that another man might even try and fuck me. I knew in my heart of hearts that I didn't want that. I didn't want a strange man inside of me. I didn't want to go that far.

Instinctively, I knew I couldn't and wouldn't go that far. I was about to walk out of the room when I realized that this could be a test of Xavier. If he had any feelings for me, he wouldn't let anything like that happen. If he loved me and cared for me, it would kill him to see me with someone else. If he loved me, he wouldn't be able to go through with this. I'd walk out before things got too crazy. And if he weren't as angry as I hoped him to be, I'd be done with him completely—100% done.

"I want all of you to go to that couch," Charles said. "We'll tie blindfolds on all of you when it is your turn. However, you can watch each other if you so wish. Does anyone want to volunteer and go first?"

"Sure," Violeta said with a silky voice. "I'm more than happy to go first."

"Okay." Charles nodded. "If you're sure."

"I am." Violeta grinned, grabbed his right hand and I gasped as I watched her stick his hand down the front of her panties. "See, I'm more than ready."

"Yes, you are." Charles grinned as he pulled his fingers out and I watched as he stuck them in his mouth and sucked. I looked at the girl next to me and she looked like she was about to pass out. I knew that Violeta was trying to psych us out. I knew that she was only going to continue trying to work us up. And I knew that she was successful already. I just didn't understand how she was so carefree and easy with her body. How could she just parade herself around like that? I wasn't sure if it was me or not. Was I a prude? Was I missing something in not allowing myself to just submit to my every whim and feeling? The other two girls and I sat on the couch and watched as Violeta got onto the bed. Charles blindfolded her and I watched as he let his fingers rub against her breasts gently before moving away. I blushed as Violeta let out a loud moan and turned to look at the door as Stephan walked in. My breath caught as he looked in my direction and smiled, his blue eyes intense and breathtaking as he stared at me. My heart raced as I gazed back at him and watched as he took off his jacket and unbuttoned his shirt. He was gorgeous and his chest was perfectly lean and muscular, like that of a swimmer.

"If you were mine, you would not be in here." He walked over to me and spoke softly as he continued to gaze at me, his eyes caressing me as I sat on the couch. I looked away and shifted uncomfortably as my stomach flipped. I felt confused and on edge as I realized that I was attracted to him. Like, really attracted to him. I wasn't sure what was wrong with me. I was in love with Xavier, yet, I was physically attracted to Stephan. In fact, a part of me wondered what he was like in bed. A part of me wondered if he was as intense under the sheets as he was in person and I hated that I felt that way. It made me wonder if I was as in love with Xavier as I thought I was.

***

"This is scary," the girl next to me said and made a face as we sat there waiting to see what was going to happen next. "I don't know if I want to do this."

"Why are you doing this?" I asked, wondering why she was going ahead after what had happened to her sister.

"I love Johan." She sighed. "I have since we were kids." She shifted on the seat.

"He's my soul mate and, well, his father said this was the only way we could be together."

"That's awful," I said, my voice sad and upset for her.

"Well, you're here too," she said accusingly. "Prince Xavier doesn't exactly have you on a pedestal."

"Well, it's not that he..." I started, but my voice trailed off as the lights went off. I was glad that the first test was about to start. I wasn't really sure what to say. What could I say about all of this?

"Let us start," Charles said and Stephan gave me one last look and winked before making his way to the bed. Suddenly some music started playing. I didn't recognize it, but it sounded soothing. I stared into the room ahead of me and watched as he grabbed a feather from a box to the right of him and walked over to the bed. He ran the feather up and down Violeta's body slowly and delicately and I could see her squirming on the bed. I felt like a voyeur as I sat there watching them and before I knew it, he was done. He walked out of the room without looking at me again and then I saw another man walking into the room. The girl I was sitting with looked down and I had a feeling that this was her Johan. He was a younger-looking man, early twenties with jet-black hair and bright blue eyes. He looked uncomfortable in his own skin and I watched as he grabbed a toothbrush from his pocket. I frowned as he walked towards the bed. What was he doing?

"Wait," I said to the girl next to me. "Why isn't Casper here?" I frowned.

"It's a test," the girl said and pouted. "If Violeta can guess that neither of the guys was hers, then Casper has a better chance of making a position in the inner circle. Most couples don't go for the double test, but I guess they are confident."

"Wow," I said and watched as Johan ran the toothbrush along Violeta's lips. I had no idea why he thought that was sexy or pleasurable and I wondered what he was thinking.

"He loves that toothbrush," the girl said softly as she peeked up at him.

"Really?" I gave her a quick glance. I wanted to ask her what she meant and if that was his personal toothbrush. Did he have a toothbrush fetish? I wanted to giggle as I thought about him cuddling his toothbrush and telling it that he loved it. I was picturing Johan kissing the toothbrush when I heard my name and I jumped up nervously. I watched as Violeta was guided off of the bed and out of a door. I swallowed hard and walked towards the bed. I guessed I was next. My heart felt like it was going to pop out of my body. I couldn't believe this was happening. I got onto the bed and Charles leaned down to tie the blindfold around my eyes. I folded my arms across my chest so that he couldn't accidentally graze my breasts. I lay back and rested my head on the pillows. They felt soft and luxurious underneath my head. I stretched out on the bed and waited, all my nerves on edge. I felt like I was lying there for hours when I finally heard the sounds of classical music playing. I waited for something to happen next. It was killing me, being in the dark. Then I felt the bed move slightly and I tensed. I felt hot breath on my neck and my body stiffened. I tried to take a deep breath and smell, but I could smell nothing but roses. The breath moved to my neck and it made me clammy all over as I lay there, waiting to see what was going to happen next. I felt the breath across my lips and then move to my ear. Then he blew into my ear gently and I felt my skin tingling. It was Xavier. I was almost positive of it as he continued blowing gently. I moaned slightly as he continued blowing and I squirmed on the bed, wanting to feel more of him on me. And then it was done. And I was there waiting again. I lay there waiting in the darkness for the next man and that was when I started panicking. What if it hadn't been Xavier? What if the next guy was Xavier? What if I chose wrong? I almost collapsed in relief as I felt the bristles of a toothbrush against my lips. It was Johan again. It had to be. I knew with all certainty that there was no way that Xavier would think that a toothbrush against the lips was sexy. I smiled to myself as I lay there, feeling confident in my answer. The bristles rubbed against my lips and it took everything in me to not turn over or push the toothbrush away from my face. This was not sexy. In fact, if every round was like this, then I had nothing to worry about. Before I knew it, my blindfold was off and I was being taken to another room. There was a thin-looking woman with a dour face sitting at a table and she asked me which of the men was Xavier. I answered without hesitation that it was number one. She nodded and asked me if I was willing to go to round two. She pointed towards another door and I got up and walked there, feeling pleased with myself.

"Hey," one of the girls who joined me about five minutes later said.

"You got Johan, right?"

"He used the toothbrush on me too." She nodded and grinned. "I'm Margerita, by the way."

"Lola," I said and she nodded.

"I know." She laughed at my surprised look and I was surprised by how much her smile transformed her face. "You're famous in this crowd. We all saw the newspapers and the engagement announcement."

"It's not real," I whispered, wanting to share something with her. Margerita seemed like a nice girl, the sort of girl I would be friends with.

"It's real enough." She smiled at me warmly. "He cares for you."

"You think so?"

"Yes." She nodded. "I can see by the way he looks at you."

"Oh?"

"When he was blowing in your ear." She sighed wistfully. "He was looking down at you with such love in his eyes. He is totally in love with you."

"Oh, I don't know about that," I protested, but secretly I was pleased by her comments. "We barely know each other."

"Love doesn't care about time," she said and took a deep breath. "I'm scared for this test."

"Oh? Why?"

"You'll see." She made a face and closed her mouth as Charles walked into the room with Violeta by his side. He had a wide smile on his face and I wondered what they had been up to.

"Are you ready?" he said and both Margerita and I nodded. I looked behind me and didn't see the fourth girl.

"She didn't make it," Charles said with a small smile as we walked into the room again. "Okay, everyone, you have to take a piece of clothing off now."

"We have to? I thought it was optional."

"This is round two. Everyone has to do it." Violeta looked at me and I watched as she pulled her panties down and flung them behind her. "Don't be a baby, Lola."

"I'm not a baby," I said and swallowed hard, trying to avoid looking at Violeta's half-naked body. Margerita sighed and I watched as she took her dress off slowly. I took a deep breath and started taking my dress off as well. I was annoyed at myself that I hadn't worn a bra with the dress. Why, oh, why hadn't I worn a bra? I was jealous of Margarita in that moment. She was standing there in a bra and panties, but then again, she must have known what these tests would have entailed. It took everything in me not to cover my nipples as Charles stared at me. I took a step back as he approached me and his eyes glittered into mine as he stopped and stood in front of me.

"You may sit down," he said as he looked down at my breasts and licked his lips slowly. "Violeta will go first again. Violeta, go and lie on the bed and I'll be there to put the blindfold on in a second."

"Yes, Charles," she said and I watched her sashaying to the bed. Margerita and I walked back over to the couch and sat down.

"You're so brave," she whispered to me as we had a seat. I could see her trying not to look at my breasts and I made a face.

"Not really." I sighed and sat back. "But what choice do I have?" I looked towards the door and that was when Casper walked in, looking smart and confident. He walked up to her and I watched as he slipped his fingers inside her legs.

"What's he doing?" I whispered to Margerita. "I thought they couldn't use their body?"

"That was test one." She bit her lower lip. "Now they can use everything, but their cocks."

"I thought they couldn't use hands in this round either?" I frowned.

"They changed the rules." Her eyes widened. "They can use their hands now as well in this round."

"Oh, my God —what?"

"Yeah." She nodded, her eyes wide. "Thank God you went braless and not panty-less.'

"Yeah," I said and closed my eyes. My breath was coming fast now. Who was going to be in the room with me, aside from Xavier, and what were they going to do? I didn't even watch Casper with Violeta; her moans and screams told me everything I needed to know. She was having the time of her life and she didn't care who knew. Then the music stopped and Casper left the room. I stared at the door, wondering who was going to enter next. In walked Stephan and this time he didn't gaze at me. Instead he walked over to the box and I watched as he pulled a dildo out and moved towards the bed. He spread Violeta's legs and I gasped as he moved her body around so that her head was in our direction. I wasn't sure why he was doing that and then I realized that he'd done it on purpose. He wanted to make me uncomfortable. He had done it on purpose to make me squirm. He held the dildo up and gazed into my eyes as he placed it between Violeta's legs. He moved the dildo in and out of her, his eyes never leaving mine. I wasn't sure why I couldn't look away. It was uncomfortable and I felt depraved, but I couldn't stop myself.

Stephan's eyes never left mine the whole time he was using the dildo on Violeta and I could feel my face growing warm. A part of my body was tingling as if he were doing it to me. I looked away then. I was uncomfortable and anxious with anticipation. What was going to happen to me?

I watched as Stephan left the room and then Violeta took her blindfold off. I was about to stand up when Xavier burst into the room, his face red and his eyes angry.

"This is enough, Lola, let's go." He marched over to me and grabbed my hand. "Put your dress on now and we're leaving," he barked. I stared at him in shock and watched as Charles walked over to us. "You do understand that by leaving you will forfeit the opportunity to join the inner circle of the Society of Brothers?"

"I don't care," Xavier snapped and glared down at me. "Put your damn dress on, Lola."

"No." I shook my head defiantly. "We came here for a reason and we're not leaving yet."

"Lola," he growled, his eyes searching mine and all of a sudden I felt like the one in control.

"Not yet, Xavier," I said softly. "You can change this."

"I don't know if I can have you do this." He shook his head. "I don't want to see another man touching you." His voice caught. "This was a mistake." His eyes fell to my breasts. "You shouldn't be here."

"I'm fine, Xavier," I muttered and I could see everyone looking at us. "Leave the room and let us continue. You wanted to make the inner circle, so let's get you there."

"Lola," he said, his voice pained, but I stood up and pushed him. I wasn't sure what had come over me. I wasn't sure why all of a sudden I felt so confident, so willing to move on to the next step. I knew that a part of me wanted to know what it was like to be pleasured by Stephan. The part of me that was still hung up on the fact that Xavier and Violeta had been together wanted to teach Xavier a lesson. I wanted to make him hurt. I wanted him to see another man give me pleasure. It was cruel and sadistic and totally true. I wasn't even sure who I was becoming anymore. I wasn't sure what had happened to the girl who had blushed at the thought of oral sex. I wanted to see what it would feel like to have Stephan touch me before the stakes got too high and I couldn't turn back. I knew it was a risk I was taking. For all I knew, Casper would be in the room with me. I knew that it was a huge risk, but it was one I was willing to take for everything Xavier had put me through. I was done being the good girl. I was done being the passive girl. I wasn't going to just let Xavier have his cake and eat it too. I wanted some fun myself. I knew there was a risk I could get carried away. I knew that there was a possibility that I might choose Stephan, but I didn't care. I didn't care because this was the position Xavier had put me in. He had lied from the beginning. I'd teach him to treat me like I was a kid. I'd show him that he wanted me; he needed to understand that I was a woman who needed respect.

"You should leave, Xavier," I said softly. "I believe I'm up next."

CHAPTER THIRTEEN
XAVIER

Lola's dismissive tone was like hot water being thrown onto my face. I was still burning in shame and anger at the way she had spoken to me, the way she had wanted to continue with the test. I watched her walking into the room and, even though her back was towards me, I could still see her naked breasts in my eyes. I could still see the way every man in the room had stared at her as she'd taken off her dress. My Lola with her breasts on display to everyone. It had killed me. I could have plucked out the eyes of everyone in the room, one by one with my bare hands. I didn't want her here. I'd made a mistake and now I was living with it. This round was going to be harder. A lot harder. I knew that either Casper or Stephan would be the other man in the room and I knew that neither of them would be holding back if they had access to her. They were going to do everything they could to turn her on. I knew without a doubt that whichever man was put into the room with her would touch her breasts gently and roughly and it made me want to puke. I was about to go and run after Lola. I was going to pull her out and demand that she leave with me, but my pride and a glance from Charles stopped me. I had to suck it up. This is why I'd come. I was confident that Lola would choose me. I was confident that I could tease her delicately without being subverse. She would choose me and then we'd figure out what to do next. I clenched my fists as I stood there and watched her getting onto the bed. Her breasts bounced delicately against her chest and I wanted to rush into the room with a blanket and demand that she cover up. I felt furious inside that she was continuing with the process. I knew that I was mad at myself, but I was also mad at her, now. Very, very mad. I was going to tease her and teach her a lesson. I was going to show her that there were many ways to orgasm and all of them weren't what she would have expected.

CHAPTER FOURTEEN
LOLA

The feather was soft, silky, teasing, unforgettable and forbidden. I shivered as I lay there being pleasured for absolutely no reason by some unknown man. I was wavering between extreme bliss and absolute panic as I lay there becoming more and more turned on. There was a certain wickedness to the excitement that I felt running through my veins as the feather ran across my skin, tickling me and turning me on. It almost didn't even matter who was in the room with me, I still felt turned on. I still felt breathless. My body felt surprisingly calm and I wondered if this was Xavier's biggest mistake, bringing me here and introducing to me a world that was both dark and exhilarating. The feather ran across my nipples back and forth and the light touch was both excruciating and mind-numbingly beautiful. I wanted to cry out for whoever was guiding the feather to just touch me. I wanted to feel the touch of his skin on mine, whoever he was. I felt captivated by the rhythmic movements across my breasts back and forth, intending to take me to the top of the highest mountain and then let me fall. My climb was breathtaking and brutalizing. The feather moved down from my breasts and towards my stomach and I felt the tip of it in my belly button and it made me cry out in shock as I felt my panties grow immediately wet. I moaned as the heat in my belly grew while the feather played in my belly button.

This was a new feeling to me. I'd never been so turned on from the touch of an inanimate object. And then the feather fell lower still and my legs spread involuntarily, wanting to give access to the feather to my most intimate spot. And I wasn't to be disappointed. Even though I still had my panties on, even though my throbbing bud wasn't being directly caressed, I still felt as if my entire body was on fire as the feather ran back and forth, rubbing a little harder against me. I spread my legs wider, hoping for more contact, but it didn't come. It was almost as if the man guiding the feather wanted to tease me and tell me off at the same time. He was holding back from satisfying me because he wanted to teach me a lesson. And then I felt his knuckles brushing across my clit as the feather moved back and forth and I could feel my climax building up even more.

"Oh, gosh," I mumbled under my breath as I felt the feather move back up to my breasts and circled my nipples. I was almost positive that it was Xavier with me in the room. He was trying to punish me for staying put and going through with the next round. He wanted to make me beg for him to bring me to climax. He was going to make me beg to have him finish the job.

"Please," I whispered softly under my breath and I squirmed on the bed as the feather worked its way across the tips of my nipples, as the sides of his fingers grazed my flesh softly. Time seemed to stand still as I lay there, feeling every brush with as much intensity as if it had been something much rougher. And then he moved back down again. And this time he didn't hold back.

The feather moved back and forth and up and down and each time I felt it soft against my panties. I then felt his knuckles, rough and determined against my bud. And with each movement, it felt more and more intense until suddenly, I could take it no more. I screamed as my body buckled with an orgasm and still Xavier, or who I thought was Xavier, continued. The feather and his knuckles continued to tease and torment me as I lay there in my own juices wanting nothing more than to be fucked. My breathing was intense as I concentrated on the light graze of his knuckles. I could picture the smirk on his face as he stared at my face and body: my parted lips panting slightly, the rise of my breasts, the widening of my legs, the curling of my toes. I was as turned on as I'd ever been. The touch of the feather, the graze of his finger, the darkness of the blindfold, the smell of sex on sandy nights, the beating of my heart, the wetness between my legs. Everything reminded me that this man had completely and utterly captured the very essence of my being. He'd captured my heart, my love, and my soul. And just like that he was gone. I could feel his physical presence leaving my side and I felt cold as I lay there. It was almost as if he'd taken away my soul with him as he'd left. My body still tingled in remembrance of his skillful touch. I could feel myself growing tired as I lay there. All I wanted to do was fall asleep, but I knew the real test was yet to come.

***

I don't know how the darkness can get darker, but it did as I lay back on the bed waiting for the next man to enter the room. I didn't know what to expect. I didn't know if I'd be even more pent up after what Xavier had just done to me. Or at least what I thought Xavier had done to me. There was still a little doubt in my mind. Had it really been Xavier? And if hadn't, what did it mean that another man had made me come with a feather and a graze of his hand?

The air seemed to change as I heard footsteps of someone approaching me. I held my breath as I waited to see what was going to happen next—if this whole process was going to be my undoing. My panties felt wet still and I wished that I'd been able to have a quick wash and change of underwear. I felt cheap and dirty lying there waiting for a mystery man to touch me. I wondered if I'd lost my mind. I wondered what all my friends back home would think if they could see me now. No one would believe me. No one would think it possible that Lola

Franklin was taking part in some sort of sexual games with the elite of Europe. I wouldn't have thought it possible, either. I wondered what Anna thought—if she was jealous of me or concerned about my safety. Most probably a bit of both. I'm sure she regretted letting me come out here by myself. We were a team. We both looked out for each other and tried to stop the other one from making mistakes. Though, as I felt the palms of the man in front of me running over my nipples, I wasn't sure how much of a mistake this was. Not if I was honest with myself. If I was honest with myself, I was loving the freedom, loving the attention and loving the wantonness of being a woman that many men desired. I felt my legs clenching as the man started to squeeze my nipples hard. He wasn't building up to anything or holding back. This man had come to turn me on and there was no game to it. No finesse or pretense. I can't say that I minded. My breath caught as his fingers ran down my stomach and straight into my panties. I squirmed as I felt him rub against my aching bud. I wasn't even sure if he was allowed to do what he was doing. I closed my legs and his fingers pulled out abruptly and I felt him rubbing my juices off of his fingers onto my panties. I lay there wondering what the man was thinking and feeling as he stood there, not touching me. I wondered what I looked like, if I looked like a whore or some sort of ethereal creature that was confident and happy in her body.

I wasn't left wondering for long because within a few seconds, I felt the man's lips on my breast, sucking gently as his tongue flicked my aching nipple back and forth against his teeth. He sucked as if he were drinking the most expensive champagne and wanted to savor the taste on his lips and tongue. His tongue was dancing on my breast in that slow, rhythmic movement that only the best dancers have. He alternated between fast and slow and rough and gentle and it was driving me crazy; absolutely crazy.

"I'm going to show you how a real man pleases his woman." The voice was gruff and unexpected as he whispered in my ear. I barely caught the words before the man's mouth fell to my breast again and he pulled and tugged on my nipples sharply, his teeth nibbling as if I were the first meal he'd had in years. I squirmed on the bed in discomfort and pleasure. My nipples were aching—in pain and exquisite delight. My body was on fire and I was aching to cry out, to beg the man to stop. I still had no idea who I was with. There had been a slight accent, but the words had been so fast and unexpected that I didn't know who they belonged to. It was almost as if the words were a part of his seduction. A part of making me lose myself completely to him, whoever he was. It was almost too much. It was as if this man had taken on the challenge of the man before. He was doing everything in his power to let me know that there was no better love than him and he was right. The pain was intense, but not too much. The pleasure hit all the right spots at all the right times. This man was a master of pleasure. He was building me up to a frenzy, making me think things I'd never thought before. Making me want to do things, to scream, to shout, to beg, to completely give myself over, just for a release. This man held power over me. He had me in the palm of his hands and that scared me. It scared me because I'd been so confident that the first man had been Xavier. And if that was correct, if Xavier had brought me to orgasm with a feather, then this meant that the man that I was currently with—the man that I'd move mountains to spend another night with—was someone else. And not just someone else, but *the* someone else. If the man with me was Stephan, with his dazzling blue eyes that had enraptured me at first sight, if that was the man driving me to this level, then I knew I was in trouble. I knew that everything I thought I'd felt, known, and believed before was nothing compared to the feelings that I was experiencing now. Heaven help me, but I felt like I was falling down a rabbit hole and I wasn't going to be lucky enough to come out unscathed.

And then because I was already waiting at the top of the mountain, he decided to send me over the edge. His teeth tugged and pulled my nipples as his hand fell to my panties again. This time his fingers stayed on the outside and he timed his movements perfectly. Sucking and pulling on my nipple at the same time that his hand rubbed against my clit, alternating between fast and slow. It didn't take me long to start moaning and screaming and it didn't take me long to come explosively; so explosively that my body shuddered on the bed as I whimpered and yet, he didn't stop. His lips never left my breast as he sucked and tugged and it was only after a whistle blew that he pulled away from me. I lay there completely spent, completely confused and completely satisfied as I was left alone, wondering who was who. Then I felt someone tapping my shoulder and I sat up, feeling dazed and confused.

"You're done." I heard the voice, but didn't see him. My mind was still on the decision I had to make. I had to decide who was the best lover; who was the one that had turned me on the most and that person would be the winner. I was terrified that I'd make the wrong decision. There was no doubt in my mind that man number 2 had been the one to drive me crazy. He'd be the one I'd have dreams about. The exquisite pleasure I had felt, even while experiencing pain had been completely new to me. It was as if he'd wanted to torment me, but to also show me just how good he was. He hadn't felt like Xavier. He'd felt naughty, dangerous, exciting, forbidden and I felt guilty as hell. I didn't know who I was going to choose. I didn't know how I was going to choose. I jumped off of the bed and walked to the doorway and exited the room. I looked around and there were was no one else in there with me. I frowned as I waited. What was going on? I stood there and a blind went up and I could see into the room I'd just vacated. The lights became dimmed and I watched Violeta entering the room again, completely naked. She lay down on the bed and placed the blindfold across her eyes. I tried to look away from her perfect body. It made me feel uncomfortable and slightly jealous. However, I didn't have time to dwell on my own insecurities because within a minute I saw Stephan entering the room. He walked like a Jaguar: regal, dignified, confident and self-assured. He oozed power and sex appeal. He was an alpha, ready and willing to take control and go with it. I gasped as I watched his hands falling to her breasts, molding them to his palms as he played with her breasts and then it was as if he knew I was looking. He turned around and looked directly into my window. He winked and then bent down and took her right nipple in his mouth and sucked. I gasped and stepped back as I knew without a doubt that it had been Stephan that had brought me to the most intense orgasm of my life. I was ashamed of myself. Ashamed and scared. I didn't know how to think and feel. All of a sudden my feelings of freeness and excitement were gone. All of a sudden I was filled with a fear and anger that I didn't recognize. I had let another man touch me intimately and I had enjoyed it. I'd enjoyed him more than I'd enjoyed the man I loved. I felt like I had betrayed Xavier. And then I felt mad. Mad that he'd put me in this position in the first place. What had he thought was going to happen? What had he expected me to do? He'd put me in this position. How could he put me in this position? How could he be okay with other men touching me? Teasing me? Bringing me to climax? How could he love me and allow this to happen? It didn't make sense to me and, if anything, it made me incredibly sad for myself. I couldn't stand and watch Stephan, either. What sort of sick fucks were these guys? What sort of world was this? Why was I here? I was just a simple girl from Palm Bay, Florida. I was a bloody Pirate, for heaven's sake. I spent my weekends at Melbourne Mall and Indialantic Beach. I went to Orlando for fun. Chili's and Applebee's were good restaurants in my world. Shit, I dated guys whose idea of fun was to take me to a football game and try and grab under my skirt during the game. I *knew* that life. I expected it, even though it had bored me. But I'd wanted more. I'd wanted an adventure. I'd dreamed of a Prince Charming and excitement, but this was too much. I wanted to go back to the days where Anna and I would drive up to Cocoa Beach and hang out at Ron Jon's Surf Shop and pretend we were surfers so we could flirt with all the hot guys in the store. I wanted to go back to the days when my only concern was whether or not my parents would allow me to go to the movies on a Friday night with a boy who'd already graduated from high school. This world I was in right now seemed too dark for me. Too scary. Too wanton and loose. I wasn't sure I could even understand what had just happened. I had willingly lain on a bed in a blindfold and allowed two different men to pleasure me. I'd lain on a bed and allowed two different men to bring me to orgasm. No, we hadn't had sex. And no, there had been no penetration, but I wasn't even sure if that mattered. Not when deep inside, a part of me was still on fire and giddy. I had ignited something in myself tonight that I didn't recognize. Something that made me question exactly who I was.

***

"Okay, it's time for everyone to make their decisions." The deep male voice wrenched me from my thoughts. I wasn't sure how much time had passed or even what I was feeling anymore. I looked around and saw that I was back in the main room. A slight jolt of surprise shook me to my core. I'd been so deep in thought that I hadn't even realized that I'd been walking and moving around. I looked at Charles as he continued talking and I wondered if he had even noticed that I was out of it. Violeta was standing to the right of me, a smug smile on her face, and I wondered how she could be so confident and self-assured. How did she not feel like a slut? I didn't understand it. Everything about this world was so different, so alluring and dangerous. I just didn't understand how she was okay with all of this. I was starting to feel sick to my stomach as I stood there. I could see Xavier staring at me, but I didn't look back at him. I didn't want to see what was in his eyes and I didn't want him to see the shame in mine. I wasn't sure who I was going to choose. I wasn't sure which man had been him. And I couldn't honestly say that both men had pleasured me greatly. Yes, man two had taken my breath away and made me weak. Yes, the pain alternating with the pleasure had driven me crazy. In my heart of hearts, I knew that man two was the one who had taken me on a ride I would never forget. But now that I was almost positive that man two was Stephan, it made me feel sick inside. Sick and twisted. I could still feel his teeth tugging on my nipple. I could still feel his fingers touching me, possessing me, making me his. I could still feel the way he'd sucked so hard that pleasure and pain had been cascading through my body as if I were on some sort of ride and couldn't get off. And then I also knew what bothered me most. I'd gone through with all of this because a part of me had wanted to see what Stephan would be like. I'd wanted to hurt Xavier, but I'd also been curious. Curious to know what lay behind his blue eyes. Curious to feel and touch him. And curious to be touched by him. I'd been drawn to him at first sight. He'd bewitched me and now he'd taken a part of me. Stephan made me realize that I was just as bad as Violeta. Who was I to judge her while I was allowing the same thing to happen to me?

"Violeta, you're up first," Charles said loudly and Violeta walked over to him, her head tall as she paraded her naked body in front of everyone. I looked around the room and saw that everyone was staring at her, except for Xavier and Stephan, who were both looking at me.

"This will be an easy one," Violeta said, her voice soft as she laughed. There were tendrils of hair surrounding her face and she looked surprising soft as she spoke. I wondered if this was the woman that the men saw all the time, as opposed to the shrew that I knew. "I know exactly who I'm going to choose," she said and I watched as she slipped her hand between her legs and rubbed her clit. My face went red and I gasped as I looked away, but I couldn't stop myself from looking back to see what she was going to do next. I watched as she closed her eyes and moaned and then just as suddenly she walked over to Casper and kissed him, before pushing her finger into his mouth. "Taste me, suck me," she cried out as Casper sucked on her fingers. "These are the juices that you produced, my darling," she said loudly. "I choose the man that was sucking on my nipples. I choose the man that made me come with one flick of his tongue. I choose the man that wanted a second chance to pleasure me in test number two. I choose Casper."

The crowd went silent and my eyes nearly popped open as we all realized that Violeta had chosen wrong. Violeta had chosen

Casper, but it had been Stephan that had gone a second time. It had been Stephan who had been sucking on her nipples. I looked over at him to see what he was thinking. I wanted to ask him why he had asked to pleasure Violeta twice. And then I knew. It was his signal to me. He wanted me to know that he'd been the one sucking on my nipples. He wanted me to be able to choose Xavier as the one who pleased me, but why would he do that? Why would he care if I chose wrong? It suddenly struck me that he wanted me to choose correctly this time because he wanted me to make it to the next round. He wanted me to make it to the round where he could do anything to me. He wanted to show me that he could completely dominate every part of me.

"You're incorrect, Violeta." Charles' voice was no longer so cheery and we all looked at Casper to see his reaction.

"Dirty slut." He sneered down at her. "Whore, get away from me."

"Casper!" she cried out, her voice pleading. "I didn't know. I thought it was you."

"Get away from me." He stepped aside from her. "Go to Stephan. He can have you now."

Violeta looked around the room manically, her eyes wild as she realized she'd messed up. She looked at Casper and back at Stephan and I knew she was trying to decide what to do. I almost felt sorry for her, but not quite.

"I don't want your sloppy seconds." Stephan's voice was almost lyrical as he spoke. "There is only one woman in this room I am fighting for." My whole body went rigid as I felt his eyes on me. "I want Lola Franklin."

"Then the slut should leave," Casper said. "Go and —"

"Enough!" a voice shouted and we all jumped and looked towards the door. "You cannot speak to Violeta that way. None of you deserve her."

"Tarquin." It was my voice that called out his name in shock. What was he doing here?

"Violeta," he cried out, ignoring me as he ran to her and pulled her into his arms. "I won't let them do this to you anymore. I won't let them pass you around. You're too beautiful, too kind, too lovely."

I almost fainted in shock as I listened to him talk. What was Tarquin going on about? Had he lost his mind? How could he call her 'kind'?

"Come away with me, Violeta," he said, his voice pleading. "Marry me. I know the family that has our beautiful daughter. We can adopt her back. We can be a real family. I'm willing to be disowned. I'm willing to lose it all. Say you'll be with me, Violeta. I love you."

I looked at Xavier then and I could tell from the look on his face that he was just as shocked as I was. Tarquin and Violeta had been together. I could barely believe it, though I felt a huge sense of relief that Xavier wasn't the father of her baby. Then again I should have known Xavier would never do that to his own child. I knew that in my heart.

"Leave me alone, Tarquin." Violeta looked at him distastefully. "I want nothing to do with you."

"But I love you," Tarquin pleaded.

"I want a king, Tarquin." She looked at him condescendingly. "I want a man that will one day be king. I want a man to possess me. I want a man that can fuck me and make me come within seconds. You—you are not any of those things. Leave me alone and scat." She looked at him coldly as she walked to the door as regally as she could. I was still in shock as she walked and I couldn't imagine how she was feeling.

"Leave, whore," Casper said and looked at Charles, who was looking like he'd just seen a ghost.

"Uhm, let us continue," Charles said and changed the subject as Violeta walked out the door. I was surprised that no one went after her. Not even Tarquin. What had just happened? I felt even more dazed and confused and then my heart lurched as my moment came. "Lola, you're next. Who do you choose as the man that gave you the most pleasure?" He looked at me curiously and I felt all the blood draining from my face. On my right stood Xavier, my love, the man I had come with and on the left, stood Stephan, eager, charismatic, handsome Stephan and he'd made it clear that he was here for me. He wanted me. He wanted to please me. He wanted to make me his. I stood there with my heart in my mouth. I didn't know who I was going to pick. I didn't know what to do. One wrong choice and my whole life would change. One wrong choice and Xavier would hate me. One wrong choice and I could be taken into a life of sexual pleasure that was far out of my realm. And the problem wasn't in the fact that I didn't know who I was going to choose. The problem was in the fact that I was going to lie. I was going to go with man number one and the feather because I was sure that had been Xavier. I was going to go with him because he was who I wanted. But if I was truly honest with myself, the man that had pleased me more was man number 2. The man who had taken me to new sexual heights was Stephan. And that made me feel guiltier than anything. I wanted to cry as I stood there, unable to speak.

"Lola," Charles said again as all eyes gazed at me. "You have to tell us now. Whom do you choose?"

CHAPTER FIFTEEN
XAVIER

I could feel Stephan's eyes on Lola as we all waited for her answer. I could see the way he was staring at her so intently, like a fox watching his prey before he got ready to pounce. He wanted her. I could see it in the way that he watched her. He wanted her and it was about more than just getting back at me. She'd touched a part of him, intrigued him as she'd intrigued me. I'd been surprised when I'd seen him with the feather, touching her lightly and delicately. I'd been sure he'd do something more, try something harder, more intimate. Like he had with Violeta. I wasn't sure why he'd used a dildo on her and then a feather on Lola, but it had calmed me down. Stopped me from going in the room and punching his teeth out. I'd been happy that he'd used the feather, until I'd seen Lola's reaction to it. It had turned her on and she'd been moaning and sliding on the bed. And I'd been crazy with jealousy and madness. And when she'd come, I'd wanted to die. I'd wanted to cut myself into tiny pieces and throw them into the ocean because it was in that moment that I'd know I was scum. The fact that I'd brought her here, the fact that I'd thought this was okay, it showed me that I was no better than the other men here. I loved Lola and I'd betrayed her and myself by trying to get into the inner circle. I knew now that it wasn't important. But it was too late. It was too late to change any of it. I was angry with myself and I was angry at myself, too. I'd lost control in the room with her. I'd lost control as I'd sucked on her nipples, wanting her to feel the pain that was ravaging me inside, but also wanting her to experience the most exquisite and tender pleasure that she could. She was my Lola, my morning glory, my colorful artwork in a room full of monochrome and I'd forgotten that. I'd gotten caught up. I wanted to punch the wall. How could I have gone down this road? We had been brought together by light, by wondrous paintings, by beauty, and I had taken her into a world of darkness and ugliness. I'd taken away our joy.

"Enough," I stepped forward and shouted. "Lola will not be making a choice tonight." I looked around the room and glared at Casper and Stephan. "I will not subject her to this anymore. We're leaving."

"If you leave, Xavier, you will be giving up any chance you may have had at gaining access to the inner circle of the Society of Brother's," Charles said and looked at me, his eyes in disbelief at what I'd just said.

"Fuck the inner circle," I growled and grabbed Lola's arm. "Fuck the inner circle and all of you. I won't do this to Lola anymore. I love her too much for this. I'm sorry, Lola." I looked into her shocked face. "I'm so sorry that I've done this to you. Please say you can forgive me?"

She gazed back at me with wide eyes, unspeaking. I could see the shock in her face. She almost looked shell-shocked. It had all been too much. I realized that now. I'd been terribly selfish and we were both going to pay for that. We were both already paying for it. "I'm done with this madness," I said as I looked directly at Stephan. "It's over," I said, my voice sounding almost hysterical. I pulled Lola towards me and walked to the door. "It's over, Lola," I said as she cuddled into me, tears rolling down her face as we exited. My heart felt heavy as we walked through the building. I had messed up big time and I wasn't sure how I was going to fix it. As we got into the car after she'd gotten dressed, I stared at her forlorn face and my heart broke. I was angry with myself and I was scared. I had made us leave because I was ashamed of myself for putting Lola through this whole ordeal, but I'd also made us leave because I'd been scared that she was going to choose Stephan. Though, I wasn't scared at the thought of not making it into the inner circle; I was scared because it meant that I could possibly lose Lola. And there was no way in hell that I was going to let that happen.

CHAPTER SIXTEEN
LOLA

There's a feeling between happiness and sadness. It's a sort of melancholy that hovers over your soul, wanting to suck you in. It's the place where tears hang out, wanting to be shed. It's the place where laughter hides, lost in an abyss of the unknown. This place is like a void, the purgatory of the living. It's a place that makes you ache, though no limbs hurt, and no painkillers can take away the numbness. Numb head, unseeing eyes, mute voice, and unfeeling heart. All of these make up this feeling. This is the feeling that I now found myself in. This is the feeling that occupied my days and made it hard for me to sleep at night. This is the place where I currently resided. I looked at Xavier and a part of me wondered at how much I hated him and loved him at the same time. How could I love and hate someone so much at the same time? I also wondered if I'd ever get out of that place. Would I ever laugh the youthful, eager, happy naïve laugh of my youth? That thought always made me smile and gave me hope. I hadn't lost my sense of humor, even through all of this. I knew that part of these feelings stemmed from the fact that Xavier hated me and the other part stemmed from the fact that I hated myself.

"What are you going to do today?" Xavier asked me loudly as he opened my bedroom door and walked into my room. He'd taken to talking to me loudly now, as if I were a hard-of-hearing senior citizen. I knew he thought that this was the only way to reach me. It'd been a week since the tests and I still didn't feel right about everything. We hadn't really spoken about what happened and we hadn't made love, either. I'd barely been able to look at him or myself. I felt ashamed of myself every time I thought of that night. I felt ashamed because I felt dirty and I felt ashamed because I reveled in being dirty in the moment. We'd attempted to talk the night he'd taken me home. I'd told him that I was going to choose him. I was going to choose the man with the feather. He'd been angry and told me that hadn't been him. He'd been the one who had been sucking on my breasts. It had shocked me and I'd told him that I had enjoyed that more, but I'd thought it had been Stephan. I'd tried to explain that I had actually preferred him more, but I hadn't thought it was him. I hadn't explained it well because it had made him even angrier. And then we'd just stopped talking about it. It wasn't something either of us had wanted to relive.

"I don't know." I sat up in the bed and looked away from his handsome face. Looking into his green eyes always made me feel guilty. I could still remember the look of hurt on his face when I told him that I'd thought Stephan had been the one sucking on my breasts that night. It had shocked him as much as it had shocked me that I'd told him the truth. I knew how hurt he felt. I knew how betrayed. I knew how confused he must have been because I felt confused as well. I'd felt like someone else was living inside of my body. How could I have had those feelings of excitement for another man?

"You should go out." He came and sat down on the side of my bed. His voice was lower now and the room suddenly became tense. "I'm going to London next week."

"Oh?" I said, my heart racing. What did that mean?

"I think we should both go."

"I see." I looked at him then. Was this it? Were we over? "So, do you still want me to be your assistant?" I asked him the only question I was brave enough to voice.

"Assistant?" He frowned. "What are you talking about?"

"You want to go back to teaching, don't you?"

"I don't know." He shook his head and then grasped my hands. "I want you to come back to me, Lola. I want brash and funny and courageous Lola to come back to me and tell me what she thinks and feels at all times. I want to be put in my place. I want the woman I first met to challenge me and hit me. Hate me if you want. Scream at me. Do whatever you have to, but please stop freezing me out."

"But you hate me." I sucked on my lower lip, my heart racing at his words. "I'm ashamed of myself and I hate that—" My voice trailed off as I stared at him.

"Stop, Lola." His voice was rough and heartbreaking in its texture. "This isn't your fault. This is all me. This is what happens when men play games, Lola." His voice was now loud and angry. "I wanted to be part of the system so I could change it, but I was part of the problem."

"I just feel like I let you down and I let myself down as well," I said weakly, still feeling sorry for myself.

"You didn't let anyone down." Xavier was almost scolding me. "I'm the one that took you there. I should have known what was going to happen."

"But I came, Xavier," I whispered and looked down in shame. I knew we had to have this conversation out completely. I knew we had to discuss everything if we were to ever move on. "I'm so ashamed of myself, Xavier. I can't even look at you," I said, my face burning as I thought back to that night again. I could still feel the way my whole body had buckled as Stephan had brought me to a climax with his knuckles and a feather. "I feel so ashamed of myself. I can barely look you in the face."

"It's not for you to feel ashamed." He grabbed me under my chin and pulled my face up to look at him. "Your body reacted in the only way it knew how, Lola. You shouldn't have been put in that position in the first place. I shouldn't have done that to you. I'm so sorry, Lola. I wish I could take it all back. I wish I could make it so none of this happened."

"Do you hate me, though? Can you ever forgive me?"

"There is nothing for me to forgive, beautiful." He kissed me softly on the lips. "It is me that needs your forgiveness, Lola. It is me that is begging you for another chance. I love you so much."

"This isn't love, Xavier!" I screamed at him as I banged my hands against his chest. "You don't love me. I'm just a possession to you. I'm just a girl you decided to use to get what you want."

"That's not true," he said, his voice surprisingly soft as he grabbed my wrists.

"You don't love me," I whimpered as tears gushed out of my eyes. I looked at Xavier and I saw his expression change. It went from concerned to sad and I was overcome with emotions. "I hate you, I hate you for doing this to me."

"I hate me, too." He nodded in agreement. "I fucked up, Lola. I fucked up bad. I got you involved in something that I didn't even want to be involved in myself. I made a mistake. A really big mistake. I don't know what I can do to make this better. Maybe it will never be better and maybe you will never trust me. However, there is one thing I know for certain. One thing I can guarantee you. And that is that I do love you. I love you more than I could love anyone."

"How do you know?" I gasped, wanting to believe him so badly, but not really believing. "How do you know that you love me? Is it because you saw another man making me come?" I screamed.

I watched as he winced and he grabbed my face again and looked at me, his green eyes looking sad and weary. "I want to take you somewhere. I want to take you somewhere so I can show you how much I love you and so you can forgive me."

I stared at him then and kissed him softly on the lips. I put my fingers in his hair and pulled him into me for a few seconds and breathed in his essence before pulling back. "I forgive you, Xavier," I said softly. "But I don't know if I'll ever believe that you really love me," I said with a sad face and jumped out of the bed. I looked down at him as he sat there, his regal face in despair and my heart sank for what had happened to us. "I just don't know if I can ever forget this," I said as tears started to run down my face. Xavier stood up and pulled me into his arms and I rested my head against his shoulder and cried. We stood there in the room, silently, his hands rubbing my back to comfort me as I cried, both for the loss of trust in our relationship and the complete and utter loss of my own innocence.

***

"Where are we going?" I asked Xavier with a confused expression as I looked out of the car window. "I don't recognize where we are at all."

"We're going to my favorite place," he said and his voice was a lot more cheerful than it had been just a few hours ago as I'd cried into his arms.

"Your favorite place?" I asked him and stared at his profile as he drove. "Your bedroom?" I joked lightly, but he didn't laugh. I suppose it was not the right time to be making sex jokes.

"You'll see," he said softly and gave me a quick look. "How was your nap?"

"Good." I nodded. "I feel refreshed." I stretched my arms and smiled at him. I took a deep breath and realized that I felt better than I had in days. I supposed that fresh air and getting out of the palace really had made a difference.

"You must have been tired," he said and I nodded, even though I knew he couldn't see me. "It's from all the crying you've been doing."

"I suppose," I said, feeling somewhat embarrassed.

"You've been crying and I've been hitting," he continued and I turned to him in surprise.

"Hitting who?" I said, my voice breathless, imagining him pummeling Stephan to the ground.

"Not who, but what," he said, his voice amused as he rounded a corner. "I was hitting a punching bag."

"Oh, okay." I felt myself exhale, though I was slightly disappointed.

"In preparation for my big fight," he continued and chuckled slightly.

"Big fight?" I asked breathlessly.

"I'm joking." He laughed and all of a sudden the tenseness in me suddenly disappeared and I found myself laughing with him.

"You see, I can be funny," he said as he pulled off of the road suddenly. "I'm glad I still have the ability to make you laugh, Lola," he said and I felt him give my hand a quick squeeze. I held on to the armrest tightly as I gazed in front of us. It appeared to me that we were driving through the middle of a field and there was no actual road guiding us along.

"I never said you're not funny," I said breathlessly as I stared at the green grass we were plowing through.

"I don't mean funny looking," he said and I felt his right hand on my leg suddenly, squeezing my kneecap.

"No one thinks you're funny looking," I said with a laugh, my hand covering his. "What are you doing, Xavier?"

"I'm taking you to my favorite place. I already told you that."

"You know that's not what I mean," I said and gasped as I saw a field full of flowers before us. Xavier slowed down the car and then stopped.

"We're here," he said and jumped out of the car. I sat there in a daze as I waited for him to open my door. I was still dazed as he leaned over and undid my seatbelt. "You okay?" he asked gently, his eyes concerned as he stared at me.

"I'm fine." I nodded, not sure why I was suddenly so overcome with emotion. "This is a beautiful place," I said, my voice breathless as I gazed at his face so close to mine.

"It couldn't be any more fitting." Xavier nodded. "A beautiful destination for a beautiful woman."

"I'm not beautiful," I mumbled and Xavier frowned.

"You're the most beautiful woman in the world, Lola. You're the blooming flower that every bud hopes to be."

"You're just saying that," I said as I blushed and stepped out of the car.

"Why would I say that?" he asked as he closed the door.

"I don't know." I shrugged and looked around. "Why are we here?"

"I wanted to show you how much I love you." He guided me through the flowers until we came upon a river. I gasped at the sight as it almost reminded me of Monet's gardens.

"This is a really special place," I said softly as he guided me towards a chair swing. He sat down and I sat down next to him.

"Do you want to know how I know that I love you?" Xavier turned to me with a serious expression.

I nodded back silently, not wanting to say anything to ruin the moment.

"I know I love you because I feel everything you feel. When you are sad, I am sad and drawn into an abyss of despair. When you're happy, my heart is soaring. When you cry, I not only want to wipe your tears away and stop the hurt, I want to cry as well. I feel everything you feel, Lola. You're a part of me. Your soul is my soul. Your heart is my heart. Your hurt is my hurt. Your love is my love. You're the part of me that has been missing all my life and I'm the part of you that has been missing. We weren't whole until we found each other. And now you complete me and I complete you. We are meant to be one."

"I, I..." My voice trailed off because I didn't know what to say. I was so captivated by him, by this place, by my emotions. I wanted to pause this moment so I could live it forever.

"Do you know why I brought you here?" Xavier said softly as he gazed at me.

"Because you love me," I said after a few seconds, the realization suddenly dawning on me that it was true. Xavier Van Romerius really did love me. For all of his faults and for all of his cockiness, he was in love with me. He'd told me, of course, but it hadn't really hit me until this moment.

"Yes, I do, Lola Franklin. I love you very much," he said and grabbed my hands. "And I brought you here because this is my favorite place in the world. This is the place I come to when I'm sad and lonely. This is the place I come to when I'm in despair. This is the place that always makes me feel better. I brought you here, Lola, because I realized that this would be the place that would provide you comfort as well. I knew that because I knew that I loved you. And I know that our love is special. I brought you here because I knew that just as I am a part of you, you are a part of me. And I knew that if you were a part of me, then you would appreciate this place as much as I do."

"Oh, Xavier," I cried out, pulling him into my arms. My heart was full and I kissed him hard. I couldn't believe that it was my Xavier saying these words. My sex-on-legs. When had he become such a romantic? And that was how I knew he was being genuine. That's how I knew his feelings for me were real and that what we had really was special. Xavier wasn't the sort of man to spout off romantic nonsense to make someone feel better. He was the sort of man who would only say such things if he really meant them.

"Oh, Xavier," I said again, gazing into his dazzling green eyes. "I love you. I really and truly love you."

"I love you too," he said and pulled me up. "In fact, I'm going to show you how much I love you right now." He leaned over and pulled my top off. "Take off all your clothes," he said and stepped back. "And then lie down on the ground."

"What?" I said, my eyes widening.

"Do as I say," he said with a smirk and I hurriedly took my clothes off and lay on the grass. It felt weird beneath my naked body. The grass was slightly cold and the ground was slightly hard, but I didn't think about that for very long. I watched as Xavier took his clothes off and threw them onto the ground next to mine. I stared up at his magnificent naked body and swallowed hard as he joined me on the ground.

"Touch my cock," he said and grabbed my hand. He grinned as I squeezed it and moved my fingers up and down. "Fuck," he growled as he grew hard and closed his eyes. "Let go," he muttered and pushed me down onto my back again. He bent down over me and spread my legs and grinned down at me.

"I'm going to show you how a real man pleases his woman," he said and I gasped as his mouth fell to my wetness and he licked around my throbbing clit. I felt his tongue flicking against it as he had done to my nipples in the room and I cried out, allowing the wind to carry my whimpers and moans to the flowers around us. I grabbed his hair and pushed his face into my wetness harder as his tongue entered me roughly, moving in and out with as much force as a cock. I could feel wave after wave cascading over my body as I got ready to come. And then he pulled out of me and rolled onto the ground.

"Sit on me," he growled as he leaned over and picked me up. "Sit on me and ride me, Lola. Show me how badly you want to come."

I looked down at his face, so sexy and gruff, and he grunted as I lowered myself onto him. I didn't play the slow-fast game that he liked to play. I immediately started to gallop on top of him, letting myself bounce up and down on his hard cock as fast as I could. I could feel his fingers playing with my breasts as I moved up and down. I screamed when my orgasm hit and I fell forward, crushing my breasts against his chest. He grabbed my hips and I could feel him still moving inside of me for a few seconds before I felt his body shuddering as he came inside of me. We lay there for a few minutes, breathing hard and holding each other, and I stroked the side of his face, feeling content. This feeling—this feeling of warmth and love—was how it was meant to be. This feeling was perfection.

CHAPTER SEVENTEEN
XAVIER

I watched to make sure that Lola was sleeping before I got out of the bed to make a phone call. I was happy that she'd loved my field as much as I had. She'd loved it so much that we'd christened it, letting our love flow into the grass as we moaned and devoured each other. I smiled at the thought of Lola riding me, the sun making her glow as her hair had blown in the wind. The afternoon had been perfect and I knew that we were back on track emotionally. There was only one thing bothering me. One thing that I couldn't get out of my mind, and that was Stephan. Stephan was the man that just wouldn't leave me. I knew that Lola loved me. I knew that I was the one that had messed everything up and nearly lost her, but I just couldn't stop thinking about Stephan. What would have happened if I hadn't taken her out of the tests? I knew she'd been attracted to him, but I didn't know if she still thought about him. I didn't know if she wished she could have seen what he had to offer. I picked up the phone and wondered if I was crazy. I had to be out of my mind to be making this call. I had no idea what I was thinking, but I knew that if I loved Lola, I had to put her first. I had to give her the option. Before she became mine forever, I had to let her go, let her make a decision that could break me. When I'd taken her from the test, I'd done it for me and her. I'd done it because I'd been scared. I'd done it because I didn't want her to have access to Stephan anymore. I was worried that he had some spell over her when he saw her. I was still worried, but I knew that if I loved her, I had to trust her. I had to let her have the option. I stood next to the wall and gripped the phone as I waited for Stephan to answer. I couldn't believe what I was about to do, but I knew that for love and for Lola, I had to make this call.

Chapter Eighteen
Lola

I woke up the next morning feeling satiated and happy. All of my worries and anger were miraculously gone. I wasn't sure how or why all of my sorrow had fled, but I was happy that it had. I stretched out in the bed and looked around, wondering where Xavier had gone. I jumped up out of bed, pulled my nightdress on and walked towards the door so I could go and look for him. I padded down the corridor wondering what we were going to do next. I could barely keep up with Xavier and his plans, but I knew I had to find out. I knew that Anna was likely waiting on my call. I wasn't sure how I was going to tell her everything that had happened since our last call. I wasn't even sure she'd believe me. I wasn't even sure that I believed myself.

I turned the corner and gasped as I saw Stephan walking towards me with a huge smile on his face. My heart flipped as he looked me over and I could feel my legs shaking as I stared at him. What was going on?

"Lola," he said, his blue eyes piercing into mine as he stopped in front of me and touched my cheek.

"Stephan, what are you doing here?" I asked in shock and then frowned. He gave me a small smile and opened the door to my left.

"Come," he said and walked into the room. I followed behind him in a daze, not even understanding what I was doing.

"You shouldn't be here," I said breathlessly as I stood in front of Stephan in the small room. He closed the door behind me and locked it. My heart started racing and I looked away in fear. "You shouldn't be here," I said again, looking at him in shock. Why was he here? And why had I come in here with him?

"Why not?" He cocked his head to the side and studied my face. "You're so beautiful, Lola Franklin, my American princess."

"I'm not your American princess," I said, feeling confused at the joy his words had brought to me.

"You could be," he said and he stepped towards me again. "Wouldn't you like to be with a man that knows in his heart and soul that you are all he needs? Don't you want that, Lola?"

"You don't care about me. This is just a game to you," I said, frowning. "You don't even know me."

"I know all I need to know," he said gently. "I knew all I needed to know the first time I saw you. It was a game to Casper and to Xavier, Lola," he said, his voice intense. "But to me… to me, it is anything but a game."

"I don't know what you want," I said and took a step back. "Please just let me go."

"You know the one thing I regret from that night," Stephan said, his voice husky as he stepped closer to me and changed the subject. I shook my head and took another step back. "You know the one thing I would change."

I shook my head again without speaking and his eyes narrowed as he grabbed me around the waist and pulled me towards him.

"Ask me, Lola. Ask me the one thing I wish I could have changed." His face was right next to mine now and he looked directly into my eyes. "Ask me." His voice was urgent and I swallowed hard.

"What?" I squeaked out, my heart racing as my skin burned at being so close to him. "What's the one thing you would have changed?"

"I wish it had been my cock that would have brought you to orgasm." He groaned against my ear as he pulled me into him harder. I could feel his erection against my stomach as he ground himself into me. "I wish it had been my cock instead of the feather."

"You couldn't have entered me." I swallowed hard. "It was against the rules of the round. You couldn't have entered me."

"I know," he said and he pulled back, muttering against my lips as he continued to hold me against him. "It would have been against the rules, but I would have entered you anyway; swiftly, deeply and all-consuming. I would have entered you and pulled out so fast that you would have almost imagined that it had never happened, except for the feeling inside of you that would have been begging me to enter you again."

"You would have been disqualified," I said, my voice wobbly, and conveniently forgetting that I'd had my panties on. Even if he had wanted to accidently slip inside of me, he wouldn't have been able to.

"I wouldn't have cared," he said. "I wouldn't have cared if I'd been disqualified or if I'd lost my crown. Not if that one moment could have changed the future. For I know, dear Lola, that once my cock was inside of you—once you felt my power, our connection, how perfectly I would have fit inside of you—you wouldn't have cared either. You wouldn't have given Xavier another thought. You would have known that I was the perfect match for you. The perfect fit. I brought you to orgasm with a feather and a knuckle. I had you moaning on the bed, spreading your legs, parting your lips, your head was feverish. All for me, Lola. All for me and my touch. If I had been inside of you, for even one second, it would have all been over. You would have been mine. Possessed. Taken. Captivated. All mine." He groaned and pressed his lips against mine softly. For a second we just stood there. For a second all I could feel was his hardness against me. All I could see was the desire in his eyes. All I could hear was his deep breathing and then mine as I stood there, my lips soft and parted against him.

"Let me fuck you, Lola. Let me take you. Give me a chance to show you that I'm the man for you." His need was guttural and the response in my belly was swift.

"I love Xavier," I said, my heart rate slowing as I pushed him away from me. I gazed up into his aqua-blue eyes and blinked. "I love Xavier," I said again, stronger this time, my voice loud and clear. "What the fuck do you think you're doing?"

"Don't fight me, Lola. Don't fight us. This is what you want. You know that in your heart of hearts. You know that in-between your legs. You know that by the wetness in your panties and the tightness in your nipples. You know your stomach is curling in anticipation, wanting to know what it would be like to be fucked by me. You know you want this. You know you've thought about me. Most likely every night. Every night Xavier enters you, you're secretly wishing it were me. Every time he touches you, you're…" His voice trailed off as he realized that I wasn't looking at him or even paying him any attention. "Lola," he said and he looked at me. "What are you thinking?" This time his voice was unsure and I looked at him pityingly as I realized how wrong he was.

"I've never once thought of you, Stephan." I gazed at his handsome face that had bewitched me the first time that I'd seen him and smiled widely. "I love Xavier.

I love him with all my heart. I love him more than anything and he loves me. I know this to be true. I know that he loves me. And, no, I don't want you. I don't need you inside of me to know that I don't want you."

"What are you saying?" His eyes flashed at me. "Are you stupid? I'm telling you that I will take you. I will marry you. I will make you mine. Even though you have been soiled by Xavier. I will still make an honest woman of you. You can have me, Lola. You can have it all. I have more riches than Xavier. More power. More *everything*. I can give you the world."

"I don't want the world, or you." I shook my head. "What you have, Stephan, is sex appeal. That's it. And all you are is sex. But that's not enough. That's not love. And that's not life. That's not anything. You can keep your sex. You can keep your erection. You can keep your panty-wetting smoothness. I don't need to be with you to know what I want. I don't need to be with you to know that I love Xavier. He is everything to me. He is my heart. He's all I need and want. But thank you for coming. Thank you for clearing something up in my mind. I was so angry with myself for what happened. I was so confused at why I'd been so turned on, but it wasn't you. It was me. I'm a sexual being. I'm a woman and I'm not going to be ashamed if I have a natural reaction. But that's all it is, is a reaction. I'm not doing anything to you. I don't want you. Do you hear me, Stephan? I don't want you."

He looked back at me in shock, his face tight. "You don't know what you're saying.

Xavier is the one that told me to come." His voice was choked and I started laughing.

"I know exactly what I'm saying, Stephan. Now get out of here." I watched as he unlocked the door and hurried out of the room. I stood there for a few seconds and took a deep breath before exiting the room. Xavier and I needed to have a serious talk, but I wasn't angry. I knew exactly why Xavier had told Stephan to come see me. He wanted to make sure that I was confident in my decision. He wanted to let me know that I still had an out. He loved me enough to risk letting me go to someone else. I loved him and hated him for it. I laughed as I ran down the stairs and looked for him. I had a feeling that this was how our relationship was going to go. It would never be perfect, but that was okay. As long as we had love, we'd be able to get through it all.

CHAPTER NINETEEN
XAVIER

The squealing of Stephan's car wheels fifteen minutes after he'd arrived made me smile. I pumped my fist in the air and then jumped out of my chair. I felt high on life and I knew that I should wipe the smile off of my face before Lola found me. I could hear her footsteps coming closer to my study as she walked and I knew that she was looking for me and was probably ready to scream and shout at what I'd done. I knew I'd been immature—stupid, even—to invite Stephan over. It wasn't even that I was testing her. I trusted Lola with all my heart. I just wanted to ensure that I was the one for her, the one that she wanted, deep inside her heart and soul.

"Xavier," she called out as she walked down the corridor and made her way to the study.

"I'm in here," I called out as I fell to the floor and grabbed the box out of my pocket.

"Xavier, you're an asshole, you know that." Her voice was annoyed as she walked into my study. Her jaw dropped open as she looked at me down on my knees, with the ring box open in front of me. "Xavier?" she said, her voice unsure now. "What's going on?"

"Lola Franklin, from the first time I saw you in London, I knew that you were someone special. I knew that you were *the* someone special. I might be a prince, and I might be your professor, but we both know

I'm still human. I've still made mistakes. Lola Franklin, I want you to know that I love you more than life itself. And I wanted to make sure that, before I asked you to be mine, I gave you every opportunity to choose someone else. I love you enough to want you to be with someone else if that was what you wanted."

"Xavier," Lola started, her face warm and her eyes glowing, "you're the only one that I want."

"Lola, you don't know how happy you make me when you say those words." I took the ring out of the box and held it up to her. "Will you marry me, Lola Franklin? Will you make me the happiest man in the world?"

"Yes, Xavier." She beamed as I slid the ring onto her finger. "I'll marry you."

I jumped up then and pulled her into my arms. "I'll look after you and protect you forever, Lola." I kissed her cheeks and her lips and she giggled as she kissed me back softly.

"And one other thing..." she said softly as her voice trailed off.

"Yes? Anything, my darling," I said, curious, wondering what was making her blush.

"Will you continue to be adventurous in the bedroom?" she said mischievously. "I kinda liked that pain and pleasure thing you did."

"Your wish is my desire." I laughed as my hands slid to her ass and slapped it quickly before rubbing it gently. "I'll do anything you want me to." She gazed up at me and wrapped her arms around my neck and I kissed her eagerly, loving the warmth of her body against mine. I knew in that moment that we could get through anything that life had to throw at us. I might be Lola's Prince Charming, but she was my forever princess.

EPILOGUE
LOLA

There are three things you should know about me:

1. I believe in love with all my heart.

2. Every night, I dream about the Prince Charming that I get to spend the rest of my life with.

3. I'm a walking contradiction.

And upon further thought, there is one last thing you should know about me. I received an envelope a couple of months ago and all it held was a feather and a piece of paper. On the piece of paper there was one sentence. One sentence that I think about every day. One sentence that I dismiss from my mind whenever it starts to make me warm and cozy or whenever it starts to make me worried and afraid. I keep the letter because as much as the writer is correct, he is also wrong. I read the letter whenever I want to remind myself of who I am and where I've been. I read the letter to remind myself that I'm not perfect. I read the letter to remind myself that life isn't black and white. Love isn't perfect and Prince Charmings are just regular men. I read the letter to remind myself that I have my happily-ever-after and that it's all I could have ever asked for. Yes, when I read the words in the letter, it makes me pause. The writer, you see, wrote one simple sentence: "In the darkness, you will always remember me." And he's correct. I will always remember him, but not for the reasons that he thinks. In the darkness, I remember the confusion. In the darkness, I remember the exact moment that I realized that Xavier was a mortal—a human being like me. That he made mistakes and I made mistakes and that was okay. As long as we could both forgive and forget. As long as we could grow. And grow we did. Yes, Stephan had touched a primal part of me that took me on a short walk on the dark side, but the memory of that walk only made me stronger. The memory of that walk made me realize that I had the best man in the world. The memory of the feather and the memory of the darkness only showed me that I'd kept the one man in my life who was right for me. Xavier Van Romerius was my Prince Charming and the fact that I'd captured his heart was the only thing that mattered. I smiled every time I saw that letter now because it reminded me of where

I'd been and where I am now. I smiled because it made me excited for my future. I smiled because it reminded me that I'm engaged **—for real this time—to marry the only man I've ever loved.** The only one who can really turn me on, heart and soul. I smile because I know that when I walk down the aisle at my wedding in front of all of my guests, including Stephan, I'm not going to be the one thinking about what went on in the dark.

NOTE FROM THE AUTHOR

Thank you for reading Keeping My Prince Charming. To be notified of any of my new book releases and to receive teasers, please join my mailing list here.

Other Recent Books by J. S. Cooper

One Night Stand
Falling For My Best Friend's Brother
Falling For My Boss